Xin Publishing

Kaleidoscope

A collection of short stories, fragments & poems by

Merrill Stenton
Leanne Moden
Anuj Wankhed
Clive Semmens
Stephen Oldroyd
Tony Gathercole
Harry Wells
Hilary Semmens
John Gathercole
Jack Stocker
Lovie Lovetree
Vince Firth
&
Helen Duff

Edited by M H He

Xin Publishing

Published by Xin Publishing
an imprint of Xin He Ltd.
83 Ducie Street
Manchester M1 2JQ
United Kingdom

http://www.xin-publishing.uk/

Text ©   Helen Duff, Vince Firth,
            Lovie Lovetree, Jack Stocker,
            John Gathercole, Hilary Semmens,
            Harry Wells, Tony Gathercole,
            Stephen Oldroyd, Clive Semmens,
            Anuj Wankhede, Leanne Moden,
            & Merrill Stenton, 2017

Cover ©   Ásta Björk Jónsdóttir 2017

ISBN: 978-3-942357-30-2

Contents

Firelight

John

I am the fire in the woods, burning bright
My light guides you to safety and to warmth.
I am the wild dance around the fire's edge,
Amidst the darkness and the rustling branch.
I am the drums that match your pounding hearts,
Quickening your steps, and rising your blood.
I am the Owl, the Fox, the Stag, the Wolf;
And I am you, your kind; children of fire;
Mine is the flame, that burns within your eyes,
The drums, and song, of laughter and of love
The flicker of my tongues the embers burn.
The fire in the woods am I; servant, friend
Your light, your warmth, your comfort and your rest
And whilst you live & breathe, & sing & dance,
I always will be there, burning brightly.

Animal Painting

Hilary

I was hanging onto Father's hands for dear life, both hands – then one hand, the other flailing – then no hands at all as I went down head-over-heels in a mud slide into the water below. Over and over I tumbled, like the uprooted trees, drowned animals and all the rest of the wreckage I had become part of. I was sucked under, jostled with boulders on the river bed and tossed back to a glimpse of sky and an anguished breath as I bounced in the flotsam roaring on down the valley. A splintered branch flipped me over, dropping me face down under a chunk of someone's gate, the last air beaten out me. Then in the middle of all this ruckus a speck of something, a little steady glow began deep inside, here in the core of me, and spread through my body, arms, legs, fingers, face, a kind of happiness. I was drowning.

At the time I was barely aware of the great flank I was thrown against, what it was I grasped, nor how we escaped the flood. It was so mixed with dreams, images of water and sky and death. And the sickness. It felt as though I was fetching up the whole of my insides, stripping away all the lining of my nose and throat with it. And in between bouts I just lay and shivered with my eyes tight shut, wishing I was dead and wondering if I was dead already and this was what being dead was like. Which set me coughing and retching again.

When at last I opened my eyes I was alone in a changed world. There were trees above me, but out to my left there was too much sky. There were no birds in it. Where were they? They wouldn't have drowned. And though I was covered in flies, why had nothing else eaten my while I lay there? I could hear faint squabbling noises so, rolling over towards the sound, I crept to where a tree hung at a drunken angle on a web of roots against the light, over an edge where I lay on my front and looked down in awe. There they all were, vultures, kites, hyenas, beaks and teeth, all glutting themselves on drowned carcasses stranded among rocks and stumps. My stomach heaved again. Far beneath me now the river was fussing away at a mass of boulders and shattered trees, trying to find a way through. I sneezed a very painful sneeze and backed away under the leafy roof.

I was naked, except for the clinging flies, no clothes, all over dark bruises and deep blue white-lipped gashes. When I put a hand up to my thumping head I found a big lump with the indent of another gash in it. I crouched there, my head between my knees, and howled for my mother, longing for her healing hands. She was never without some salve or other of herbs to ease hurts like these. And something warm and comforting in the pot – I felt a fierce pang of hunger. There was no sun but it was broad day and we'd been sitting down to supper already when we heard the first wall of water roaring through the combe. I must have been under these trees all night. Untouched.

It hit me that my family must all think I was dead. I had to find them quick and put their minds at rest. But where was I? Everything was so changed. I had no idea how far the water had carried me. I looked at the skyline – it seemed familiar – or was it? I had never seen that huge slash of raw rock and earth down it before. Perhaps it was a different peak. But wherever I was, if I followed the river upstream I was bound to get home in the end.

It was too dangerous to venture onto the ground below the high water mark where I could see the water, so when the trees gave out I had to force my way through the scrub. The rain had killed the scent of the bushes, but as I chewed on leaves and twigs to numb my hunger the biting, heady flavour was still powerful. The going was terribly heavy, though, sometimes the bushes were as tall as me and their stiff twigs tore at my bare body with all its cuts and bruises till I grizzled out loud, pushing through and grunting. Why could I find no paths? It was a relief to get under trees again, where the undergrowth was not so fierce. Had all the paths been on the lower levels where the flood has scoured everything away? I crept to the edge once more and stared down to where the river, shrunken again, was now backing up and ponding behind the massive blockage it had put in its own way. Caught in the branches of a broken tree there was something spread-eagled – it looked like a person, a child. Strings of long black hair. It couldn't have been my brother – could it? There were other black-haired children in the world. I turned my back and blundered on, retching and coughing.

Whether I liked it or not, my thoughts would keep rattling along. The sound of that first roar rang in my head, over and over. It had made us all jump to our feet and rush outside, just in time to see the wall of water coming through below us like a stampeding herd, carrying off our bridge like a child's stick boat. I could it inside my eyelids, between me and the sky, everywhere and forever.

"Twice the height of a man," wailed Old Auntie.

"But we are ten times the height of a man above it," came Father's deep voice. He explained how there must have been very heavy rain in the high country, and calmed, we all went back out of the wet to our supper. He could never have guessed how our river, our merry little river, could cut away its banks and undermine everything. My mouth had been full when a noise like the end of the world shocked us all outside again, to see the first three houses collapsing down into the water. That was my grannie's house – gone. The scream I gave then still echoed in my head.

Image after image – the houses twisting, falling in on themselves, so slowly, then gone altogether in the blink of an eye. The people running, Mother calling me. The ground opening a deep crack under me, a while length giving way. Myself slithering with it. Father's hands, desperately clutching, slippery with mud. The smack of the water, its weight suddenly on top of me. A mash of branches. The white air. Arms and legs suddenly spread, buoyant as wings, as suddenly crumpled. Dark – light – dark – light – lost – lost…

I pulled up short. I was on a path, not a human path but trodden deep by hooves, big and small, cloven. Cattle. Another picture shouldered in and once again I felt the great heaving flank I had been thrown agains, its coat rough on my numbed skin. My hands had grabbed at it of their own accord, slipping on the water-smoothed hair. Something had hit me on the shoulder, hard – I looked and saw the deep gouge it had made – somehow I had clutched it – a horn, a huge horn – then the pictures dissolved in a mess of memories of pain and cold and vomiting, everything spewed up, heart and all. I was sick again, with nothing to bring up. My sore skin crawled, blue and goose-pimpled.

There was clear water bubbling from the moss at my feet. I fetched a deep, painful breath, drank from my cupped hands and forced myself to go on, so raw inside and out that everything was blotted out except how I wanted my mother.

I couldn't help feeling I knew where I was now, though it looked all wrong. Ours was only a little combe, tucked away between big friendly hills. The little river that gave us water for drinking and cooking and washing and playing in cut quite far down through it; you had to go down a lot of steps to reach it or the sturdy wooden bridge linking us with the other half of the village. But it was only narrow. There was just an enormous gorge down there now, awful. And yet when I looked the other way, up the hill, surely that was the crooked pine my brother and I had climbed to get the young falcon, just ready to fly, for our uncle to train. I looked back in disbelief at the desolation below. Then I began to run distractedly about, my movement jerking animal-like cries out of me. There was the path up to where the bilberries grew, but when I turned to see its other end it was gone. There was the place where we had found the yellow woundwort for Mother that time when Father's hatchet had slipped. There were the two rocks leaning together that my little brother called his "best house." But where was the road home? Where were the houses?

Where were the people?

I howled for them. They had to be somewhere. I called and called till my voice, already hoarse with all the crying and sickness, was squeezed into a strangled squeak and finally stopped up. I found nothing, no-one, only the stealthy sounds of the night beasts beginning to stir, for this day too was coming to an end.

The Painter found me in a wheezing huddle right in the middle of the path from the village to the Painted Cave. He took me in his arms and carried me to his living place under the crag, where he wrapped me in soft shawls and fed me with savoury broth from the pot slung over his fire. For a long time we didn't talk. I just sat in a nest of wool – Mother had knitted it for him the winter before – and warmed my hands round the cup, staring into the flames, while his voice caressed me with meaningless crooning. At last I slept.

Gradually over the next days I learned that the whole village and all the folk, all my dear dear folk had been engulfed in the landslide, all but the Painter, who had been up here in his workshop. And me. In the end I told him my story, bit by bit as my heart let it go.

He began to understand how I had been saved.

"It was a bull?" he asked.

"I think it must have been."

"A bull came and you rode him out of the flood?"

"Something like that."

"And when you woke he was gone?"

I nodded, puzzled.

"Come," he said, getting up and lighting his torch from the embers of the fire. Wondering, I followed him into the Painted Cave, past the first part where the children were allowed and on into the narrow places where we weren't supposed to go. Sometimes we could only get through by crouching, even crawling. Sometimes we climbed down slippery rocks or squeezed round corners where I couldn't see the light and had to grope my way. Once I hit my head on something that made so lovely a sound I stopped dead. The Painter came back for me.

"It's only my bells, music from the Old Ones," he said. "They hang down from the roof. See? We're nearly there."

And then we were in the holiest place, the Painted Place. Deer leapt out of the shadows on the walls, their antlers flaring as the light caught them. There were men, wolves… I wanted to stop and look but the Painter with his light was still going ahead and I had to follow. At last the light found what he was taking me to see, my bull, my great, strong beautiful bull, with wide horns, so wide and glorious – and there was I! On his back, clutching his horns, my hair spreading in strings all about me! I began to shiver and sway, black dark washed over me. The Painter steadied me with his arm and my sight cleared.

"This is what I was painting when the flood came," he said.

"So that is why the bull saved me?" I thought of all the people who had perished. And only I was saved. It was unbearable. His eyes held mine. "Why me?" I croaked at last.

The Painter looked at me, his kind face gaunt in the wavering light.

"You must be needed for something special," he said.

We stood there a long time, wondering, and then we turned back to the painting. The torch flickered and then burned brighter. The bull moved, grew red and huge, tossed his head. My painted imaged tossed her head too. I felt the wind of his gallop in my hair, his warm strength between my knees. Then the light dwindled and the painting went back to the shadows on the wall. I drew a long breath.

"How do you make the pictures?" I asked.

The Painter regarded me gravely. My dearest of men. "I'll teach you," he said.

And that is how I became the first, perhaps the only woman painter ever. Mostly I painted the Bull, for it was he who brought our new tribe into being. And he has sustained it in good times and bad, so that our children and grandchildren and great-grandchildren have flourished all my long life through.

Ginny Tickler

Harry

She had a wheelbarrow
A plain square box
With long wooden handles
And bicycle wheels.

She had a beautiful face and a woolly hat.
Fourteen, sweet, innocent and mute.
In the words of the era,
She was not all there.

She collected vegetable parings
A war-time measure to feed pigs.
When she saw children playing
She would stop and wait and smile.
Always on the edge, looking through
An invisible curtain at a fairy story.

Boys would tease though not hurtfully.
The girls would say, 'No! Leave her alone'.
They understood more.
Once only, I touched her finger tip
Through a sheet of glass.
And loved her across the divide.

She went home one dark afternoon,
Taking a short cut by the canal towpath.
They found her body face up in the water
Surrounded by floating potato peelings
That should have been rose petals.

Will she be there with other angels
In a place where the barrier has been lifted,
The haze removed and clarity restored?
I hope so. There are things I need to tell her.

Only yesterday I thought of her and I know
That I will now be the only person left
Who has known or will remember the grace
And purity
Of this beautiful child.

Bunker 2.1

Stephen

Last Time in The Bunker – The world ended. Fortunately Colin, a council cleaner with a green thumb, Howard, the Night security and part time blackmailer, Desmond, a low grade council flunky and Mary, the PA of a less important flunky, were all able to get to the Bunker. That's as concise as it gets, if you want to know more then read *Bunker* in *Different Minds Different Lives*, what are you doing reading this first anyway? Google it or something… sheesh.

So you may be thinking, 'Ok, fair enough it turned out to be needed, but that's an awful lot of money to spend on something that spent the vast amount of its time doing nothing.' But you'd be wrong. All of the RECC facilities were in almost constant use. Just not for what they had originally been designed for.

It has now been a little over a month and our dwellers have settled in. Desmond has moved into the Bunker Commander's suite and has been spending his time liaising with RECC1. He feels this puts him in a better position when the inevitable changes come down. He was the first of the dwellers to start using a Bunker uniform and is more than happy with how it looks. But then it was designed to be flattering for the more middle-aged man.

Colin, well let's be honest nothing much has changed for Colin. In fact Colin's life has become, as far as he's concerned, discernibly better. He no longer has to spend any of his time half-assing a job he hated. He agreed, after a short argument with Mary, to open a second hydroponics unit and grow things other than just dope. As it transpires, he has a knack for it and he has found a deeper level of satisfaction than he can ever remember having. About the only thing he's really missing is online porn.

Mary on the other hand has an awful lot of aggression to get out of her system. She has spent much of her time in the senior officers' gym and on the shooting range. She too has discovered she has a knack. When she isn't running off her aggression or blasting paper targets she has begun to learn the ancient computer systems of the Bunker. In turn the Bunker's super computer has enough of a learning facility that it has recognized its preferred user. Yes, I said super computer. And yes, it can learn. No it is not artificially intelligent, it's just very cleverly programmed. But well get back to that later.

Finally Howard. Howard has had something of a working class epiphany. He has been spending his time exploring the bunker. At first this was just to keep himself away from the other dwellers but slowly his sense of morality was piqued. This started when he began to explore the third class accommodation. Initially he was horrified at the barrack-like living quarters. Cramped rooms with multiple bunks. Then he found out that the standard food ration for these quarters was a nutrient rich paste. But what really caused him to rediscover his working class ire was when he realized that his security key could be used to not only lock the barrack rooms but also deny them essential resources, like air. So it's rather a shame that this new realization on his part is about to be ripped away and the old Howard will once more be the loudest voice in his head.

Mary is having a chilled day. In part this is because she has been sneaking the odd spliff but mainly she has had a good day in the gym followed by a decent scoring session on the firing range. She sits with a warm post exercise glow and idly flicks through various commands on the computer. She isn't even bothered by the lack of a GUI today although her hand still twitches towards a non-existent mouse.

As she sits there a warning flashes up on the screen.

Attention: Detention Centre food supplies nearing critical

For a moment she simply reads and rereads this without really taking it in. Then two things occur to her. Firstly that there is a detention centre and secondly that its supplies are dwindling. Naturally she assumes this is due to degradation. She considers this for a while and then takes advantage of the computer's more responsive system and types

– Why?

It would be churlish to suggest, by the way, that her ability to use the computer was in any way enhanced by her occasionally being stoned. Churlish, but accurate.

Detention Centre Supplies have been Critically Eroded by occupant

She has also become used to the computer's seemingly random use of capital letters.

She quite naturally asks the only question that makes any sense.

– What Occupant?

Prisoner number 053

So once again we are going to be privy to information the Dwellers do not know. After the events of 9/11 the various intelligence forces found themselves in a bit of a fix. Some of the terrorists that they had acquired could not be moved around in the open or, more importantly, be questioned in the open. In this case 'Open' meaning anywhere that people gave a damn about human rights. Several solutions eventually got utilized the most egregious being extraordinary rendition. But where do you put these ghosts in between their trips across the borders? Conspiracy theorists of course came up with an excellent and interesting theory about hidden prisons. And in the case of England at least they were almost right. Both MI6 and the CIA remembered that they had extensive and highly secret prison systems prebuilt and scattered around the country. They had in fact been using the Bunker Detention Centres to 'Disappear' people almost since they were finished. Just not quite as much as they had recently.

In Zahid's case he had been in RECC6 for several months. This was, he was forced to admit, a step up from some of the other places he had been held, if for no other reason than he hadn't as yet been subjected to 'Enhanced interrogation.'

He had originally been snatched on the border between Pakistan and Afghanistan some 3 years ago. His captors insisted he was a highly trained Al-Qaida terrorist. He insisted he was a British National on holiday who had been out with his cousin trying to buy some weed. It probably didn't help his case that the American team that had snatched him could not understand his thick Brummie accent. His translator too had issues with this and the MI6 agent who had been brought in to assist was, unfortunately, a West Brom fan.

Zahid is not in fact a terrorist. He really was just trying to score some Afghani black. He's also not quite the Muslim that his father would like him to be, although his appearance of faith has been markedly improved since he was forced to spend time with, in his words 'Religious nutjobs.'

When he hasn't been terrified for his life in the interrogation rooms he has been terrified for his life in the prison common areas. In fact his time in RECC6 has been thus far comparatively relaxing. He's even occasionally been able to watch someone play computer games and movies on his in-cell monitor. He'd still quite like to know how Villa are doing however. There will soon come a moment when he realizes everyone he knows is dead and he will feel guilty when his first thought is 'I will never see Villa win the premiership.'

Us

Leanne

We are indefinable
Unkept promises and unwritten love letters
Overdue library books left on petrol station forecourts.
We are a fraction, divided by zero
The movement at the edge of the Venn diagram
Spit spat onto hot pavements.
We are your final warning and your very last chance
We are dead celebrities and living politicians
The smell of rotten vegetable matter, tobacco and raw meat.
We are not quite one thing or the other
A window shattered by the body of a bird
The stringless guitar strumming silent melodies.
We are woodsmoke and wanderings
The scent of sex in stained sheets
A three course meal in a shitty restaurant.
We are cyclical arguments
A long-lost sibling with too many memories
Rusted padlocks on a chain-link fence.
We are the tip of your tongue and the back of your mind
We are everything and nothing
And that's just the way we like it.

The Saint and the Goblin

John

On the northern edge of the Westmorland village of Heymanceaux is the parish church of St Nian – one of the oldest churches in the North West of England. Church records suggest that it was built in the 11th century on the ruins of an older hermitage; that of St Nian of Donniegenny. St Nian was said to have come to the area 300 years earlier from a monastery in Ulster, to preach the gospel to the inhabitants of the area; and was known as a fearless foe of the old ways. There are several stories told of his exploits in the area – and sometimes from further afield as well. There is at least one story of his connected with the site known as Weylands Tree Circle to the south of Manchester. But in the main his stories are centred on his exploits in the moors; wrestling giants and outwitting bogglings. One story – first written down in the seventeenth century – has an especial bearing on the church.

It was said that as St Nian was walking along the path from his little hut to the coastal village of Buddhaven one day, he was stopped by a goblin, who challenged Nian to prove that Christianity was better than the old ways. Thinking quickly, St Nian proclaimed that Christianity was so superior, even creatures such as the goblin knew its worth without realizing it. The goblin scoffed, and demanded proof. St Nian told them that the next sentence that the goblin uttered would be from the Bible. The goblin laughed and said that this was as impossible as the sun rising in the west. Quickly St Nian told him that very phrase was part of Verse 4 of Chapter 12 of the Book of Mallachrias. He said this with such conviction and holiness that the goblin believed him – even though the holy man had made this up on the spot. The goblin stomped off, swearing to leave St Nian alone, and allowing him to continue on his way.

That evening St Nian was walking back from Buddhaven when the goblin confronted him again, He had realized that he had been deceived and wanted revenge. Goblins in folklore – like all fairy creatures of that ilk – are always bound by rules and honour. The promise he had given meant nothing as it had been given under false pretences. The goblin declared that he would get his vengeance for the deception in full measure, an eye for an eye and a tooth for a tooth. Triumphantly St Nian interrupted, for this time he could clearly and truthfully say that the goblin had quoted from the Bible: the Gospel of Matthew, Chapter 5, Verse 38.

The goblin was furious, but this time he could feel in his bones that the holy man had spoken the truth. Nevertheless he demanded from the saint recompense for the lie that had first been told. St Nian agreed that this was only just. He told the goblin that his home and the hill it was under was theirs, and that the church would never have a claim upon it. Satisfied the goblin left the holy man in peace to continue on his way.

So the old story goes.

In 1849, an accidental fire destroyed the vicarage of St Nian's parish church. The incumbent at the time, Reverend Joshua Meldrum, decided that instead of rebuilding on the burnt out site he would have a much larger vicarage constructed, at a location just outside the village called Hob Hill.

However, the work went badly, with foundations being washed away by unseasonable rains, and freshly constructed walls collapsing overnight. Bricks and slates would go missing from the stores, only to be found scattered about the base of the hill the following morning

More inexplicable were the symbols that appeared on the outside of the wall of church's north side, that looked like broad scratching daubed with paint. No matter how much the wall was scrubbed, the markings could not be removed, and always seemed in the morning to be as fresh as if they had been put there only the night before.

Disturbed, Reverend Meldrum consulted a fellow clergyman and local historian, the Reverend Thomas Halliday. Halliday had a consuming interest in the folklore of the region, and knew of the story of St Nian and the Goblin. It was clearly nonsense, he told his colleague, but perhaps some of the more superstitious of the parishioners might not agree. Reverend Meldrum concurred, and decided to alter his plans and build on the original site of the vicarage after all.

That night, the markings on the church wall disappeared, and in the morning a neat and tidy pile of bricks and slates were found on the site of the old vicarage. Reverend Meldrum never found out who was behind these obvious pranks; none of his parishioners ever claimed responsibility.

Thomas Halliday referred to this story in his book, "Folklore of the Lakelands," noting how the story of the Saint may have inspired what was obviously the actions of the villagers. He even provided an illustration of the graffiti that had been daubed on the church wall, as a curiosity.

It was only in the 1990s when Dr Terrence Rollkin, the anthropologist who did so much to bring Thomas Halliday's work into public prominence, realized that the markings shown in the illustration were familiar. In a paper to the British Anthropological Society he was able to show that what seemed like random scratchings were characters of the ancient Celtic script of Ogham, a method of writing not used in the British Isles for at least a thousand years.

It was in fact two numbers, he stated: five, and thirty eight.

The Land of the Midwinter Sun

Clive

I live in a town called Toptown. It's called that because it's very nearly at the top of the world. Mummy says the world doesn't really have a top, but everyone knows it does really.

My Mummy is a Scientist. My Daddy says he's a Scientist too, but Mummy says he's really an Explorer, and that that's why he's away from home so much.

Our teacher told us that the stars you can see in the sky in winter are really very big, they only look little because they're a very, very long way away. She told us that they're just like the Sun, except that some of them are a bit bigger than the Sun, and some of them are a bit smaller. She said that maybe some of them have worlds like ours spinning around them, just like our world spins around the Sun.

She told us to imagine that there might be little children just like us on one of those worlds that there might be spinning around one of those stars. She told us that we couldn't possibly send a letter to them, and they couldn't possibly send a letter to us – but she said we had to *imagine* that we could send letters to them, and get letters from them.

She said that their world was probably very different from ours. Maybe it was much hotter, or much colder, or it had more land and less sea than our world, or more sea and less land, or maybe it didn't have any sea at all. Maybe it rained all the time, or maybe it didn't rain at all. If it didn't rain at all, they wouldn't even know what rain was!

I think our teacher must have been talking to my Mummy, because my Mummy talks like that, too. Other people's Mummies don't talk like that at all at all.

Our teacher told us we had to write about our world as though we were writing for one of those children who might be on one of those worlds there might be spinning around one of those stars. "And remember, they don't know anything about our world yet."

So this is what I've written.

Our world is mainly sea. People can live on the sea in boats, but most people spend most of their time living on land. The land we live on is the biggest island. There's a lot of other islands near ours, some quite big and some small. Beyond that, there's lots and lots of sea, then further away there are some more little islands. Then a long, long way away there are more big islands – even bigger than our island – but they're funny islands. I'll tell you more about them later.

Long, long ago, people didn't know the world was round, and they didn't know about the faraway islands – they only knew about our island, and the others nearby. They had little boats to get from island to island, and to go fishing. They used to go quite a long way out to sea for fishing, but never so far that they couldn't see the land. They didn't want to get lost.

Oh, that's another thing Mummy told me about. You know how in Winter the sky's black, and when it's not cloudy you can see stars; and in Summer the sky's blue when it's not cloudy, and the Sun goes round and round the sky; and in the middle of Spring and Autumn the Sun comes and goes for a week or two, without it ever really getting dark? Well it's not like that everywhere. Mummy says that the further away from Toptown you go, the more the Sun goes up and down. If you go far enough – she says you've got to go right out to sea to really see this – the Sun comes up for a little while every day even in the middle of Winter, and goes down for a little while every night even in the middle of Summer. She calls it The Land of the Midwinter Sun, which is silly, because it's not land at all, it's out at sea.

Well, as time went by, people built bigger boats to go fishing in, and they caught more fish. If you've got a bigger boat, you can have a taller mast, and with a little girl – or boy – at the top of the mast, you can see further, so you can go further away from the land without losing sight of it. But you still can't go very far away from the land, and you're sure there are more fish further out, and you want to get them. So somebody worked out how you could find your way back home even when you'd gone out of sight of the land. Then people started going further and further away from home, looking for more and more fish.

And they found more islands! That *was* a surprise. Even more surprisingly, there were already people living on some of those islands – funny people, who couldn't talk. Well, they could talk to each other, but they couldn't talk properly, and although they could understand each other, no-one else could understand them, and they couldn't understand anybody else. And they lived very rough lives, and wore very rough clothes and lived in very rough houses and had very simple boats, and no bicycles and no schools and no books or pencils and only a few very simple tools made from wood, bone or stone. No metal.

But that's a very long time ago, and all those people have learnt how to talk and how to live, and life on those islands is very like life on our island now, except that they're a long way away. Oh, and they *are* The Lands of the Midwinter Sun.

Now I've got to explain The Land of the Midwinter Sun to my star-circling friend. I'll worry about that later!

Most of those other islands are very little and they're a very long way from everywhere else, but Mummy says some people like living there anyway.

Then further away still, there are more islands, and some of them are very big – you remember I told you about them, and said I'd tell you more about them later. Well, now *is* later. There were people living on some of those bigger, further away islands, too – but not actually very many, because although the islands are very big, only a little bit of some of them is any good to live on, and even those little bits aren't very good to live on really. Very unhealthy and uncomfortable.

The liveable bits are very hot and steamy, and there are lots of strange insects and strange animals. Some of the insects are very big and scary, and some of them – little ones as well as big ones – have really nasty bites, like a mosquito bite only much, much worse. You can get very ill, or even die, from an insect bite down there in The Land of the Midwinter Sun! Some of the animals can bite you to death, too, Daddy says. I don't know why he wants to go there.

Mummy says he's really more interested in the places beyond the liveable bits.

Beyond the liveable bits it gets hotter and hotter, and the Sun comes and goes more and more, until you get to the fattest bit of the world. Daddy says that at the fattest bit of the world, the Sun goes up and down like crazy. Every night, even in the middle of Summer, you can see the stars; and every day, even in the middle of winter, the Sun goes right across the middle of the sky! And it's ever so ever so hot. You can't go outside the ship for very long at all or you'd be cooked, Daddy says. It's only since they invented cooling systems – like a big fridge for a whole ship, only not really cold, just cooler than outside – that they've been able to go so far.

And those big islands really are big – they stretch all the way to the fattest bit of the world and beyond. But they're just bare rock and sand, mile after mile after mile. People have got out of the ships and gone and climbed on the rocks and walked on the sand, but not for long. It's too hot.

Then after the fattest bit of the world, it starts cooling down again. It's still horribly, horribly hot for a long, long way, but eventually it gets down to temperatures where you can go outside for a while, and then cooler still and almost reasonable. And then finally the land isn't bare rock and sand any more, and there are forests on the land, a bit like the hot and steamy forests on our end of the big islands.

By this time, Daddy is thousands and thousands of miles away from Toptown – getting near to Bottomtown, in fact. Except that there isn't any Bottomtown, because there aren't any islands at the bottom of the world, it's all sea.

And down there at the bottom of the world, the temperature's nice again, and the Sun goes round and round the sky properly just like it does here, except that when it's winter here it's summer there, and Daddy's never been to the bottom of the world when it's winter there and summer here.

And then there's the biggest surprise of all. It's all sea right at the bottom of the world, but there's lots of land not so very far from the bottom of the world, close enough to the bottom of the world that it's not too terribly hot, and there are people there, too. Quite a lot of them. And they can't talk, either – well, they can talk to each other, but Daddy and his friends can't understand them, and they can't understand Daddy. That's just like the people that were found on the islands not so very far away from home, but in other ways they're not like those people. They've got good tools, and books that Daddy can't read, and roads and carts and things, and altogether quite an advanced society. And Daddy says there's lots we can learn from them, and lots they can learn from us – once they work out how they can talk to each other.

But I should tell you a bit about Daddy's main interest. Daddy's a geologist. He looks at rocks, and tries to work out how they got to be the way they are. There's lots of geologists, and between them they've worked out an awful lot. They've worked out that the world is ever so, ever so old.

Which I think is funny. Surely the world just IS? Hasn't it always been here? How can the world have had a beginning? How can the world have an age, like a little girl, or even a grown-up? But never mind about that. I'll tell my star-circling friend about what Daddy thinks, not what I think.

They've found fossils of creatures that lived long, long ago, that were completely different from anything that lives nowadays. Some of them were amazing! That was millions of years ago, they reckon.

But one of the most amazing things is that much more recently, only thousands of years ago...

Only thousands of years ago? My Daddy is funny sometimes. Thousands of years is a long, long time.

...they think that the world was much colder than it is nowadays, and that Toptown was buried in ice. Ice miles deep. Can you imagine that? The world like a great big fridge. Rain falling from the sky frozen solid! Even maybe the sea frozen solid. Nobody could possibly have lived anywhere near Toptown. But people lived in a lot of those places that are too hot nowadays, Daddy reckons. Well, lots of Daddy's friends reckon that much, too.

They've found bits and pieces of things that they think those people long ago must have done, here and there on the coasts all the way to the fattest bit of the world, and a long way beyond. They reckon those people long ago did some pretty fantastic things, but most of the things they've found are pretty hard to understand. Daddy says thousands of years can mess things around rather a lot, and it's quite hard to work out what the things they've found must have been like before they got messed around.

They're pretty sure that there'd be a lot more things to find if they could explore further inland in the bare rock and sand places. Or if they could dig deep under the sand, there'd probably be interesting things there, too, because the sand gets blown about by the wind and buries things, and in thousands of years things can get buried very deep. But they can't get far away from the sea, into the middle of the land, and they can't dig deep, because it's so very, very hot there.

But what Daddy is thinking, he says, and what he's trying to get his friends to think about too, is that because of all that ice on Toptown, and another lot of ice he says there must have been on some of the islands down near where Bottomtown isn't, sea level must have been much, much lower than it is now. And lots of those people long, long ago would have lived on land that's under the sea now, and maybe there were a great lot of them.

He says that quite a few mysteries might be explained if there were billions of people for a few generations, all that time ago. Just imagine – billions. Hundreds of times as many people as there are now – thousands of times as many as there were just a few generations ago. He thinks that when the world was colder, all those big islands that are now too hot to live on, and mostly bare rock and sand, must have been good places to live. There'd have been plenty of room for lots more people – billions, even.

Only Daddy doesn't call them people, he calls them *proto-humans*. He says people must have evolved from a few of them who survived some kind of big disaster – something that heated the world up a great lot. I like the world how it is now, but they must have thought it was quite a disaster all those thousands of years ago.

The next story is from her Daddy's point of view...

Wild Speculation

Clive

"I must admit that's what it looks like to me, too. But we can't publish anything based on such flimsy evidence. Looked at objectively, it's little more than wild speculation."

"Can't we? Lots of groups publish stuff that's no more solid than this – less solid in some cases, if you ask me."

"We've got our reputation to think of. Some people certainly do seem to get away with publishing things like this, but I can think of a quite a few groups who've damaged their careers beyond repair like that. It's not a risk I'd take lightly."

"But if we don't publish, we'll continue to be the only group looking at it; and with the evidence being so thinly and randomly scattered, the odds are that working on our own we'll never find enough."

"It seems randomly scattered, but perhaps it's not really random. Perhaps we can think of a way to predict where we can locate it. We ought to put some effort into that. I understand very well what you're getting at, but I don't want to risk our reputation unless we really have to."

"So. What do we have? Let's tabulate it and put our thinking caps on for a while. Start with what we actually know for sure."

"That's actually less than we might think. Some important pieces of the jigsaw are the work of other groups, whose conclusions might be less securely founded than we'd like."

"You're both being risk averse. Don't just think about the groups who've ruined their careers by publishing something speculative that turned out to be wrong. Think about the groups who've succeeded big time by publishing something speculative that turned out to be right. More to the point, think about the vast majority who slave away and never get anywhere because they don't publish anything until after someone else has already published."

"But no-one else is working on this, so that won't happen to us."

"Can we be sure of that? The big error the groups who spoil their reputations make isn't publishing too soon, it's clinging to their ideas after they're disproved. If you're open from the outset about how speculative the idea is, and you're ready to abandon it if it turns out to be wrong, where's the risk?"

"It's not as simple as that. There's psychology to think about. People are naturally sceptical of other people's ideas, and they'll regard an idea as untenable even if you don't; they'll think you're clinging to a disproven idea long before you're ready to abandon it. You don't succeed big time by publishing something speculative that is actually correct and then abandoning it as soon as anyone pooh-poohs it. On the other hand, you don't save your reputation by not abandoning an idea that turns out to be wrong until years after everyone else has ridiculed it. That's not simply a difficult balancing act. There isn't actually any space between the two problems at all. They overlap. It's always, inevitably, a gamble."

"And if you don't gamble, you can't win. It's just a matter of making sure the odds are as good as we can make them. Okay."

Unconformities are some of the most interesting things in geology. They form a gap in the geological record for the location, because rather than deposition occurring at that location, the surface was being eroded – meaning that not only is some old record being destroyed, but also no new record is being created for a period. But the state of the erosional surface itself at the time of the change back to deposition gets recorded – and that can be especially interesting.

In general, most deposition occurs under the sea, and land surfaces are mostly being eroded. Deposition on land does occur, particularly by water in the lower reaches of valleys, and by wind in deserts – but we think such deposits are often short-lived, and deposition and erosion occur in cycles over long periods. Thus many unconformities represent the state of the land at a time of sea level rise.

According to our theory, sea level is pretty much at an all time high at present, so that almost all the unconformities we can find – without trying to engage in underwater geology! – are in rocks that have been uplifted. These are all very old unconformities, and while they're interesting, they're not the most interesting of all. There are a relatively large number of them, and the erosional surfaces they represent have been widely examined. The interpretation of these surfaces is relatively secure.

The unconformities we have been investigating are those very few newer ones, formed above sea level since the beginning of the current period of high sea level, which had been tentatively dated to about 12,000 years ago. The deposits above the unconformities are mostly unconsolidated sediments, either river-borne or windblown, or, in a few places, volcanic ash or lava flows.

A couple of months later, we decided we were ready to go public and take the chance. It fell to me to present our ideas at a conference.

"Several lines of evidence suggest to us that about 12,700 years ago, a species of creatures very similar to ourselves – indeed, most probably a species from whose survivors we have evolved – underwent a population explosion, followed unsurprisingly by a population crash. At their peak, they may have numbered half a billion, possibly even more. We believe that a wide range of previously unexplained mineral aggregations with interesting chemical characteristics and sometimes with odd geometry on a variety of scales may be the remains of their extraordinary activities."

"Much of the world's surface has been remodelled by natural forces since that time. Much has been eroded away, and most of the rest is buried under more recent sediment. Only in a few places are these interesting aggregations at the surface, but presumably many more have been lost to erosion or are beneath sediment elsewhere. And of course that species, even with a population of half a billion, didn't cover the whole surface of the Earth with the remains of its activities anyway, so the majority of locations even where the surface is of the appropriate age are devoid of them. In particular, for reasons that will become clear, they may mostly have lived in areas of the world not now inhabited."

"You're doubtless familiar with Peterson's idea that, at some point in the past, the Earth was for some unknown reason considerably colder than it is today; that sea level was approximately seventy metres lower than it is today because the water was tied up in a great depth of ice on land at high latitudes; and that land at lower latitudes was cool, wet, and forested. We know many of you see difficulties with this interpretation of the evidence. However, we believe Peterson's suggestions to be broadly correct."

"One of the main lines of evidence for this is the existence in many places around the world's coasts, of an approximately level platform seventy metres below sea level, which is remarkably similar to the wave-cut platform at low tide sea level today. We would like to see more depth soundings around coasts in areas of the world where they are currently sparse or absent, to confirm or deny the existence of this platform elsewhere."

"We suspect that deposits similar to those we have been investigating may be present more frequently under the sands of tropical deserts or under the sea, in most places under many metres of mud at the bottom of tens of metres of water."

"We have reason to believe that, whatever the reason for the change in temperature of the Earth, it was approximately contemporaneous with the rise and fall of that species. Further investigations are required to determine whether the temperature change occurred just before the population explosion, presumably causing it, or just after it. So far the evidence points to the latter, suggesting, difficult as this might be to believe, that the temperature change may have been a result of the population explosion."

I was challenged on several points by speakers from the floor, most of which were issues our group had already considered and where necessary investigated, and which I was therefore able to answer reasonably well.

The question of the variability of the exact depth of the seventy metre platform was raised, and of course we didn't really have a good explanation of that. Peterson's suggestion is that the bedrock may have moved vertically in response to the changes in ice and seawater loading. We are fairly sure that bedrock does move vertically, during mountain building for example, but it's hard to believe that such movement has occurred significantly in a period of only 12,700 years.

One young woman had a very interesting contribution to make.

"This ties in well with something our group has been working on. Lake sediments in several places in the world show clear annual variations in particle size and composition, enabling us to date the layers precisely. In addition, they show a complicated but consistent pattern of variation from year to year. Several trace elements and compounds show a clear peak at about the same time everywhere, tailing off exponentially thereafter at different rates. We don't currently have any site anywhere in the world that covers the whole period, but by matching up partial records from different lakes or fossil lakes we have managed to make a pretty convincing montage of worldwide particulate deposition from the atmosphere. We had quite independently arrived at that 12,700 year figure for the peak."

She went on, "Recent variations from year to year can be clearly associated with particular volcanic eruptions, and most of the older variations seem to be of a similar character and we tentatively associate them with earlier, undocumented eruptions. The 12,700 year peak is of a markedly different character, involving a radically different spectrum of elements, and in particular several organic molecules that as far as we can ascertain are found nowhere else in nature. The length of the recognizable tail is much longer, due to the greater residence time in the atmosphere of some of the materials involved."

We are still waiting to see whether we will be proved right or wrong, or whether, even if we are right, anyone will believe us. Extensive excavations under hot desert sands haven't proved feasible, and it's difficult to persuade sailors to measure the depth of the sea in locations where they have little interest in the information themselves. Evidence is mounting, however, and it now seems likely that the peak population of these proto-humans may have been as high as ten billion, and that they may have inhabited a substantial percentage of the world's land area, far more than is habitable today.

Bunker 2.2

Stephen

Snaking through the corridors and passageways, which don't mean the same thing at all, we return to a slightly fitter looking Howard. While he hasn't as yet started wearing the Bunker uniform, he has taken to paying closer attention to his appearance. Perhaps spending as significant amount of his time with a gun in his hand has reminded his muscle memory about a few things. He would never admit it but part of the reason he has been exploring on his own is he caught himself just in time to stop saluting Desmond. His pace has become once more that languorous half march that soldiers the world over use to cover the distance between pubs.

As we find him he has in turn found something interesting. Perhaps not in the grand scheme of things, but interesting none the less. He has found the Garage. When it was built it was considered that it could also be used as a parade ground. That possibility was abandoned early on but not before the decorators had made a pass. Thus the garage had a jaunty paint scheme and a high ceiling that gave the whole room a feeling of space. Once the lights had shown him what he had found Howard was initially confused. A manifest discovered in an adjacent machine shop had led him to believe that the Bunker's full fleet would be lined up in military fashion. Instead he found a massive parade ground with four, what were clearly vehicles, under sheets in its centre. They hadn't even been rolled off the lift that stealthily popped up in the Town Halls sub level carpark. Pulling off the first sheet he grunted to find a military land rover that had in all likelihood been built before he was born. Same again under the second sheet. The third was a little more surprising. It was a Lord Mayor's Rolls that Howard clearly remembered being replaced a few years ago. But the last sheet held the prize, as indeed the laws of drama demand. A pristine Jaguar E-Type. He looked at it for a while. Then he checked the manifest. Then he spent more time looking at it.

– What the fuck is this doing here?

He glanced around the hall a little self consciously. Then with a possessive pat he replaced the sheets. As he was fondling the sheet covered Jag Mary's voice bounced around the garage as each speaker seemed a little out of sync with the next.

– Everyone get to the Command Centre. We have a guest.

After a moments confusion Howard grunted again as he decided to ignore it.

– Actually I really only need Howard.

Howard's shoulders slump slightly but then he perks up and walks to the nearest communication unit. He considers for a moment just ignoring Mary or just turning up. But he has learnt a thing or two about Mary these last weeks and knows she will just keep talking till he responds.

– On my way up.

Of the two remaining Residents it should come as no surprise that Desmond both gets to the Command Centre first, and was only encouraged to speed when he heard only Howard was needed. It's not that he's suspicious by nature. That's more a habit one picks up in town council politics. It's more that Desmond is crushingly bored.

His communiques with RECC1 are rare and chillingly familiar. In the past when he was bored at work he could browse the internet. And not just for porn, oh no, Desmond was active online in many ways. He had been rather shocked to discover quite how much of his day had been taken up with social media. In desperation he had gone to Colin.

Desmond – What other entertainments are there down here?

Colin had considered the question for a moment. He looked at his freshly lit joint and raised an eyebrow at Desmond. Desmond's frown cowed him instantly.

Colin – Well theres the library. Its got a video section, only current up till '85 though. There was a brief pause which hung in the smoky air.

Desmond – Go on…

Colin – Oh? Er.. Well I've got some good games for my PS, you look like a Football Manager type to me.

This got him another raised eyebrow.

Colin – Well just look through yourself later then eh? Erm, You could try talking to the computer?

Desmond – What?

Colin – The computer, it's pretty smart. I mean it's not Jarvis or anything but it can hold a conversation. Kinda. Desmond furrowed his brow and shook his head.

Desmond – An AI? An AI in a bunker under a Town Hall?

Colin – Well no it's not…. Its not Intelligent in that sense, it's just been…. Written in a clever way. I guess without a GUI interface they had to do something to make it interesting. I'd go mad staring at screens full of text all day, wouldn't you?

Curiosity piqued, Desmond went for a look-see. It's hard to adequately describe the Bunker's Super Computer. That's what it is, or rather was. When it was built it was a massive achievement. Its counterparts in the other Bunkers had all been linked to later form the spine of the UK's internet, but not this one. It is tenuously connected but the required upgrades never applied. As the years passed the splendid machine became more and more mundane and for the most part forgotten. But when it had been first created some thought had been applied to its everyday use. The primary consideration being 'How are non-computer people going to use it?' And this proved to be quite a quandary. Sadly, while it is an error to generalize, seventies computer people were the kind of people you would expect them to be and so the solution was obvious. Get it to talk.

Wolf

John

The wolf looked at me, and I stared right back – exhausted. I was leaning against a tree – I could feel the rough bark rubbing through the thin material of my shirt – and my legs felt like they could no longer carry my weight. Breath came in short, sharp & painful rasps, and my entire body was starting to shake.

The wolf, in contrast, seemed hardly winded by our chase. It had run me down for who know how long through the woods; never completely in sight, but always ensuring I was aware of its presence. It looked at me calmly; a gaze that I somehow could not avoid.

And now it had stalked silently out of the undergrowth and stood just yards from me. Terror hung between us; it was going to kill me, and I was going to die. There could be no possible other ending to this chase.

How do you describe the feeling when you know that death is almost certainly only seconds – and less than a few yards – away, and there is no hope of escape?

How do you face up to something that seems so inevitable; knowing that you will never see you loved ones and friends again?

How do you ignore the stench suddenly coming from your trews and the wetness that is running down your leg – so scared you are?

How do you think rationally?

Perhaps you don't.

With a scream that was half courage and half articulated terror I sprung away from the tree, directly at the wolf. If I was going to die, perhaps I would not die alone. Instantly the wolf also leaped towards me, sensing that the game it had played was finally ending.

We met on middle ground; my hands desperately grasping at the wolfs throat, its jaws snapping at mine with far greater strength than I could muster.

It was a hopeless struggle. And yet... and yet... I still fought.

As we rolled over and over on the ground, and I finally felt the teeth closing around my neck, I caught the expression on the wolf's face. For an instant it seemed that I was seeing a human face rather than a wolfen one; a face that seemed at once ancient and yet timeless. And then all I could see was the wolf's head, filling my vision.

A hot pain exploded within my head and chest; and all seemed to fade away. My body felt heavier and heavier and as an overwhelming urge to sleep ran through me, I heard a voice. Quiet, and loud, soft and rough.

"Yes. Yes, you will do."

And then, all was darkness.

Music

Hilary

It was stifling inside the little sled house. Vigdis was getting such a big girl now that however he twisted and flattened himself, Egil could find no way to lie down without her grumbling and pushing at him. The mountain summer was drawing to its close. When they could see the sun, which lately they often could not for the turf-hugging clouds, it went under the line of the sea for quite a while each night. It would soon be time for their father and uncles to round up the sheep and cattle and take them back from the high pastures to the farm a hard day's travel below.

Not that the men were far away. They slept in the stone shieling on the far pasture but they checked every day to see where the flocks had got to, milk the ewes for the cheese to carry back later to the village in the valley, and move the little sled house on its wooden runners to the sheep's new position. It was only at night that the children were responsible for watching that nothing bad was happening, that no wolves or bears were threatening their animals. Crammed in the little sled house they slept fitfully, on the alert for any unusual sounds or changes in the light nights, and all they had to do if wolves did arrive was to to whistle for the men to come with their weapons and drive them off. The children stayed snug and safe in their little wooden house.

Nothing much happened to disturb the tedium of that bright summer. Egil and his sister were at daggers drawn. The grown-ups often said, sniggering, that many a marriage was begun in that little old sled house, but not, Egil thought savagely, when it was your own big sister and she was getting uppity about where you put your elbows and knees in her soft bits. At least they kept each other warm if the nights got chilly, but tonight, after a blazing hot day, there were no sharp fingers of air through the peepholes to give them relief from the heat. Everything was so still and it had gone unnaturally dark. No sun, no moon, no stars, no sky at all. Lying there so closely tangled with his sleeping sister that he was drenched with her sweat, Egil was deeply uneasy, almost too uneasy to be resentful of her heaviness.

The sheep were restless too. He squirmed round to apply himself to a peephole but he could see nothing. A cold wind poked him unexpectedly in the eye and he sat up, cracking his head on the wooden ceiling. Vigdis woke up, cross.

"Oh for gods' sake!" She shouldered him roughly against the wooden side. "What do you think you're doing?"

"I'm going out," said her little brother, tears of pain brimming on his lashes. "I'm sick of being squashed. Anyway, the beasts are a bit upset and I want to see what's going on."

"Well, be careful, that's all. If you get into trouble it'll be me that gets the hiding." A gust of wind banged the sled door behind him and shrieked out through the peepholes. The sodden patches where Egil's body had been pressed against her were suddenly chilled and, shivering, Vigdis drew herself together, broad awake now and anxious in the darkness.

Egil stumbled against a sheep and crouched there listening, his fingers burrowing into its fleece. The ewe was still lying down, but her head was up and he could hear her breathing just below the threshold of a bleat. The weather really had changed. Another gust strong enough to make him stagger had flying needles of ice in it and set the sled house rocking and creaking. Some gust, that! You'd've though that hulking great Vigdis was heavy enough to hold it steady. He couldn't see the sled house now but he heard the door open.

"What are you doing, Egil? You know you shouldn't be out there. Come back at once!"

Who are you to be ordering me about, he muttered rebelliously. Then, aloud, "The sheep are beginning to get up. I want to see what's got into them."

"Don't you dare! You bad boy! Just whistle for Dad if you're worried!"

Egil felt a thrill of wickedness. Without answering he turned and pushed into the rising wind. Vigdis's whistle shrilled through the darkness. Stuff Vigdis. By the time Dad and the uncles got their things on he could be halfway to meet them. Sheep were getting to their feet and pushing at each other as he forced his way between them. He felt encumbered, then upsettingly mobbed. They were pushing him off course. "Dad!" he shouted. "Dad!" He pivoted, straining eyes and ears. Then, with gladness, he heard men's voices and turned in their direction, pushed his way through the milling fringes of the flock and began to run. Dead Grandad's voice came sharply into his mind: 'Never run on a mountain unless you can see a clear half mile ahead or you might not be able to stop.' He pulled up, obediently, unsure where he was. For a moment the wind dropped. Wrapped in black silence, he could hear his heart beating. His voice when he shouted again seemed thin and bodiless, but there were the men's voices in answer, though very faint and far away this time and in quite the wrong direction. How had that happened? Loki is leading me, he thought, frightening himself so much that, forgetting wise Grandad, he broke into a run again, fighting the wet darkness. He pitched over an invisible snag of rock and rolled down a long way, clutching at tussocks of harsh grass between stones until he fetched up against a boulder, bruising his shoulder and hip. He crouched there whimpering as another slash of hail hit him and, pulling his tunic close round himself, he hankered for Vigdis and her suffocating sticky heat. It was a relief to be out of the wind but this time his quavering shout brought no reply. He could hear his heart beating again, a tripping, stumbling beat – he must be ill – not frightened, no, a true son of the North must never be frightened – but the regular dancing beat was oddly comforting. Struggling to his feet, he tried to work out which way it was that he had last heard the men's voices and, seeking for each step with outstretched hands and probing feet, he began to climb. His heart was quiet again. The Ave Maria came into his mind – he had no idea what the Latin words meant, but he knew their power – and he moved to its rhythm instead, repeating it over and over as the priest had taught him. An ever-present help in time of trouble, the man had promised. Maybe it was the holy words that stopped him, foot in air in the pitch dark, and sat him down instead of letting him walk over the edge of a cliff and fall the gods knew how far. He sat there shivering and thinking while he got his breath back.

This was not the way he had come. Creeping on all fours, feeling for the edge, he came at last to the shelter of two big rocks leaning companionably together. Dawn could not be far off. This was as good a place as any to wait for it, so he made himself as comfortable as he could and closed his eyes. As he drowsed he could hear his heart, that same strange beat, in patterns as regular as they were intricate and changeable, now slower and deeper and then high and quick, stirring the blood. How could that be? It was a strong beat, not like a fever. He put his hand on his chest. The sound was not there – it was in his head, deep inside him. Had some spirit possessed him? Such things had happened, Grannie said. His hair stood on end. He curled into a ball, covering face and head with tight arms.

The beating stopped. In its place an unearthly sound filled his head, an angel – or a devil – a singing so unbearably sweet it hung in the folds of the mountain, touching him with a lingering caress, soaring and fading, swooping suddenly back to kiss him and then melting away. The beating began again, its pulse subtly underlying the singing. Somehow comforted, he slept.

The storm had gone. Egil opened his eyes. Rosy light was beginning to finger the undersides of lines of clouds in a sky like white violets. He looked about him in the pre-dawn light. Behind, the rocks, above, the mountains. Below, a small lake, bleak, ringed with black stones, and there on its pebble beach was a group of cone-shaped dwellings, ragged poles sticking out of the top through a hole they shared with a curl of smoke. The smell of meat cooking reminded Egil's stomach of breakfast. He could make out a stocky figure coming out through a flap of a door, a creature – woman? – child? – tiny man? – in a bulky coat and trousers and a cap with earflaps already glowing red in the strengthening light. The – person – was fetching water from the lake in a wooden bucket. A reindeer lay there, tranquilly. He knew reindeer. They competed with the sheep for forage in summer, but they were wild, magical animals, with fearsome antlers and huge hooves. Lying there, tranquil? No-one could get near them. No-one knew what happened to them in the long black howling nights of winter, when nothing mortal could live on the mountain tops. Where did they go? Or were they not mortal? Demons, even? And these people – were they people? – who lived in friendship with the reindeer (there were more of them along the lake shore, he saw) – who were they? And what were they?

A child came out – a girl? – in a short blue frock over trousers, black hair fanning over her shoulders, and stooped down by the reindeer, her arms around its neck. Someone else came out and tidied the child's hair before tying a red cap over it with strings under the chin. And then the person coming back with the bucket of water began to sing. His heart, his own heart, the one in his chest, leapt and quickened. It was not the same song, but it was the same voice, sweet, vibrant, unearthly. The hairs prickled on the back of his neck.

Where was the beating heart? Did it come out of the air? Or did these beings have a way of making it? If he could find out how it was done, could he learn to do it himself? Ah, these new figures coming out of the

house door – house? – they must be men, bigger than
the others and more handsomely dressed. The strong
blue of their tunics and the vivid colours of the
decoration on them and their high, splendid hats
glowed in the young sunlight. One of them looked to
have a wide silver belt with a knife – no, two knives
stuck in it. Could they really be as small as they
looked? Not much bigger than he was himself, these
strutting, magnificent men, half the size of his father or
Uncle Sven. Was it they who tamed the magic
reindeer? Made the heartbeat music?

He was too young and alone to meddle with magical
people, but one day, one day he must find the answers
to all these questions. Cautiously he eased his sore,
stiff muscles into motion and edged away, keeping as
quiet and as much out of sight as he could, glancing
back often at the group by the lake, until at last he lost
them to view over a brow. For a long time he fancied
he could still hear the fairy singing, and the beat of the
dancing music made its way into his movements,
lightening the labour of the journey.

Now, at the top of the mountain, where hail still lay
in sheltered streaks, he began to recognize where he
was. Away on a far pasture he could see clustered white
blobs of sheep and little men like sticks circling them.
He put his head down and forged doggedly in their
direction. There was going to be the grandmother of all
hidings when he got back; all the same it would be
good to be with his family again.

But he had heard the magic music. It still rang
through him, body and soul. Had he really seen the
musicians? Or had he just imagined he had, in the
dying dawn light? A dream? Made of nothing but cold

and fear and the ache in his bones? Whatever it was, he knew the music was real and he would spend the rest of his life looking for it. And finding a way of bringing it out to people from where it now lay, beating in his head and his heart and running in his blood.

The Mercy Machines

Jack

02:15:01
Harlem Court, Black Sector.
Kilo Team on-station.
Attempting to establish live link…

…

…
Established.
Network Hub acknowledges. Kilo reports mission critical resource acquired. Operative relays:

– Barricade didn't hold up particularly well, did it Cherry?
– He's just a civilian. He couldn't have known better.
– Ooh, what's that?
– Paperwork, Mother. It's his.
– Oh. Boring.
– I'll just be a second. Don't go anywhere.
– …
[Records received. Updated.]
– …
[Minor aural disturbance.]
– Leave it alone.
– …
[Records received. Updated.]
[Further disturbance. Likely glass fragments.]
– Mother!
– I'm bored!
– Just hold on a minute!

– We're wasting time.

[Image received. Filed. Records received. Updated.]

– We've been over this; Hub needs the info and I need the pictures.

– And if the Skurms walk in while you're scanning those?

[Image received. Filed.]

– Hub said there aren't any Skurms left in the building.

– What if there are?

– Then we follow procedure.

– Oh, this is such bollocks. The Network should have separate teams for this bit.

– Jesus Christ... Have you done any Tac-Analysis?

– No.

– Stop sulking and do some Tac stuff.

[Aerial remote access request. Hub acknowledges. Granted.]

– Yes, well. The last Skirmisher cleared out from Harlem Court at 23:04:07. They infected five people, leaving them all in the building. The Wade family succumbed and destroyed each other at about midnight, and another poor mare walked off her balcony at 01:42:03.

– Which just leaves Sam.

– Infected at 20:04:54, which gives us about ten minutes to get to him. He'll already be dead by now. So are you ready?

[Image received. Filed. Profile complete.]

– Yes, done.

– Right, finally. I've run through all the scenarios and in all of them you're going to have to work pretty blooming quickly, Cherry. We don't have time for the full song and dance.

– Got it, Mother. I'll do my best.
– We have no Asimovs on-station, and aerial is RTB, so keep your wits about you. Right now, it's just you and me.
– You know I wouldn't have it any other way.
– Don't get sarky with me.
[Entrance access. Kitchen. Operative breaching…
…
…
Optics flare. Needle sensors triggered: Movement.]
– SKIRMISHER
[Tracking]
– CHERRY, HIDE
– MOTHER, DON'T R
[Channel cut. Kilo Team dark. Hub is attempting to re-establish…
…
…

When they left, they left the lights on.

Sam wants to turn them off, but he can't. He can't move his legs. He can feel the Reaper sliding through his veins like oil. What bits of his skin that he can see have already turned black. His chest feels cold, and he tries not to look down at it. They tore holes in his shirt as they stabbed him with the syringes. Sam can still remember the face of the closest one, giggling at him through broken teeth, one hand clawing at the strips of flesh hanging from beneath its left eye. Its darkened skin, pockmarked with puncture wounds. An ear was missing, and what was left of its hair looked like it had been glued to its head.

Sam can still see it so clearly.

He wants to turn the lights off.

It would be easier in the dark. It would be like hiding. He feels exposed, vulnerable. And his home... he can't stand to see his home like this. As some of them injected him with the Reaper, the others tore pictures from the wall, smashed electronics to the floor. They burned his clothes and books, including his wedding photo album and the dress he'd bought Isabel for her birthday. Any food left in the kitchen was smeared over whatever they couldn't smash, and when they ran out of that they used whatever fluid they could coax from their own ruined bodies. When they were done, they turned on one of their own and tore him limb from limb. Their victim laughed along with them as he was eviscerated, as if they were all privy to the funniest joke in the world.

Then they left him to stare at it all, as the Reaper slowly kills him. Reanimates him.

He wants to turn the lights off.

Sam hates himself. He should have had tools, a plan. He wants to scream, but his throat is burning already. Even if Izzie and Hannah get back here safely, they'll only find this. Him. Or – the thought makes him want to be sick – maybe he'll be a Skurm already by the time they get here. God. He tries not to think about it. He should have just told Izzie to head for the evacs. They're long gone now.

What has he done?

He can hear noises. The skittering of legs against tiles. Low humming, like the buzz of wings, getting closer all the time. Sam feels himself tremble. Maybe it's the Network. He remembers hearing one of their aerial drones outside, as the Skirmishers pumped the Reaper into him.

He spares his arm a glance, and looks away again immediately. But it hurts. That's good. It hurts. He tries to hold onto that. He remembers the buzzing of the drone again. It was close. They must have seen. The Network are coming. They have to be.

From behind the door, there is a thud, and then a screech. The skittering noise gets closer.

Sam wants to turn the lights off.

[Live link re-established. Kilo Team reading.]
– It's just a body.
– Then why the fuck was it *moving?*
– It was leaning against the door, Mother. It must have just bumped it when you swung it open.
– Has it got a head? I'm not coming any closer if it still has a head.
– I promise you it's as dead as they get. Even if it isn't, it doesn't have any arms. It's perfectly safe.
– You and I both know that is an extremely relative term.
– OK, you stay there then.
[Medical analysis initiated...]
– Are we sure he wasn't armed?
– He's a civ. Why would he be?
– Echo Team found A-Sec weapons in the homes of two supposed civilians a few hours ago.
[Archive access: Assigned Security Records.]

– Nope, he wasn't A-Sec. All the weapons in this block have been accounted for anyway.

…

…

[No new data.]

– Well, Sam didn't do this, A-Sec or not. Clan kill. Maybe ritual.

– I'll take your word for it.

– I don't understand why you're always so jittery. You're the one with the firearm.

– That's why I'm carrying, isn't it? Can we move on and shut this door again, please?

– It's not going to wake up, I promise.

– Whatever. Our time is ticking down, Cherry.

The pain is gone now. Sam is afraid.

He can hear the horrible, rhythmic tapping of their many legs against the wooden floors. The muffled thumps as they reach the carpet. He hopes that whatever is on the other side of the door is carnivorous. Maybe they will kill him before the Reaper completely paralyses him. He worries that they won't have time to get in here before it takes him over. The room already seems darker, as his vision starts to tinge with black. Yes, this would definitely be the best time for them to tear his throat out. He wouldn't feel anything.

He tries not to focus on his legs. Or his arms. The fact that he can't move them. Even lifting his head takes a Herculean amount of effort. He doesn't want to become one of them.

The tears well up from somewhere inside him, but they have nowhere to go. His tear ducts have closed up, his eyes ballooning as they turn marble-black. The lights that seemed so bright before, get darker still. He knows he has to keep his head up. If he can keep his head up, he's alive.

He only sees the door. It opens slowly, pushed from the other side.

Something curls a tendril around it.

– Holy hell, we have even less time than I thought.

– Mother –

– Cherry, look at his eyes!

[File transfer. Sclera darkened, pupils and irises intangible. Advanced stage.]

– He needs –

– No. Get started.

Two creatures crawl slowly into the room. They are the size of large cats, or small dogs. The closest one moves towards him on eight segmented legs, the glimmer from the fading lights sliding liquidly from its long, ellipsoid thorax. A thin, catlike tail whips slowly from side to side behind it, while a fine line of brilliant purple light flashes from the optics of its rounded, upturned-pyramid head. It crawls forward, slowly but purposefully. The other one stops a few steps back, tail swishing, its own optics shimmering blue-green. It rears up slightly, nervously clicking its front forelegs together. Sam cannot see the black cylinder swivelling on an axis, just beside its head.

The closest one stops, just beside his knee.

"Sam?"

Its voice is soft, melodious and perfectly sexless, in the way that only a synthetic's can be.

He barely has the strength to nod.

"Sam, we are Network machines. Do you understand why we're here?"

He opens his mouth to speak, but his throat has closed up. It pads cautiously onto his lap, laying two forelegs against his heart.

"Don't talk, sweetheart. Listen, I'm sure you know this, but I'm afraid you died some time ago. The Reaper stopped your heart. I have to be quick – we don't have long before it starts to fully reanimate you. I'm sorry we couldn't get to you sooner, and have a proper conversation."

He blinks. It's about the only thing he can do.

"I am the MM-549D *Cherish Loved Ones*, and my twin is the MM-472A *Mother of Necessity*. We are here to prevent your transition to Skirmisher. Mother is monitoring you, and assures me I have time tell you some things. The first is that we, the Network, have intercepted your wife and daughter. Network Asimovs reached them before they entered the Black Sector, and they were evacuated three days ago. We're sorry we couldn't get to you in time."

Sam wants to laugh, or cry, or shout. Or do all three. But he can't. His body isn't responding. The panic tries to rise, but it can't get hold of him. Izzie and Hannah are safe. They're safe.

[File transfer. Timer display.]
– Thirty seconds.
– Yes, *alright*, Mother.

"We're working on all this, Sam. I promise you, the Network will sort this out."

The *Cherish Loved Ones* rears up, filling what's left of his vision. It lays a foreleg on his face.

"You waited for them. We're proud of you."

Then it disappears, transferring itself to the floor. Sam doesn't see it. He can only see the image it's projecting into the air in front of him. The *Cherish Loved Ones* has salvaged it from the wreckage in his hallway, and it's the most intact one it can find.

Izzie and Hannah smile at him.

They're the last thing he ever sees.

Bunker 2 – Interlude

Stephen

Programmer 2 – It bloody did!

Programmer 1 – I assure you it bloody didn't.

Programmer 2 – It asked 'What am I'

Programmer 1 – And again, no it didn't. It didn't ask anything, it reacted. That's all it can do.

Programmer 2 – Well yes I know that but it just asked that out of the blue, don't you see?

Programmer 1 – That it's doing what its programmed to do? Someone asked it that question and now it is using its expanded vocabulary. Bloody lucky it didn't run it through the thesaurus first.

Programmer 2 – Look that was a perfectly natural mistake…

Programmer 1 – Perfectly bloody obvious I'll agree, but still

Programmer 2 – And I still say we are going to have to think about regional accents.

Programmer 1 – Because the computer will clearly be dealing with lots of Scousers and Geordies

Programmer 2 – Gandalf

Programmer 1 – What?

Programmer 2 – Gandalf… we erm… me and the boys thought…

Programmer 1 – No!

Programmer 2 – Well we have to call him something.

Programmer 1 – It, we have to call It something. How about what it is, The computer? Or perhaps we should be polite, Mr Computer. Or Miss even, Then we could call it Eliza Doolittle.

Programmer 2 – Well… Eliza's not a bad name for a

Programmer 1 – Shut up. Anyway, regardless of its name, it does not think.

Programmer 2 – But that's the whole point isn't it? What we are supposed to be trying to achieve?

Programmer 1 – No, it really isn't. That may be what you lot fantasize about. But I assure you it's merely been filled up with lots of existential nonsense to Wind you Up. It is not aware. What it is, is bloody useless.

Programmer 2 – Well we have been making headway with the Sub Commands for entry level users but it doesn't like that.

Programmer 1 – Pardon?

Programmer 2 – Well it keeps crashing out when we try and compile a definitive list.

Programmer 1 – It doesn't like it?

Programmer 2 – No, we were doing ok, but then you said we couldn't play music while we worked and He's been grumpy.

Programmer 1 – Are you sure you're cut out for this kind of role?

Programmer 2 – Oh this is my dream job sir!

Programmer 1 – Indeed. Look, I will make this perfectly clear for you. We are Programmers. We program. We are not magicians who create life with a wave of their hand. We are not dealing with the birth of a new age of awareness, we are trying to make a complex machine simple enough for a government employee to use. Nothing More. So no more 'Gandalf' nonsense.... Oh dear, that's why the main server has a wizard's hat on top isn't it? I want less fantasy and more reality. If you continue to anthropomorphize the damn thing we will never get anywhere. So quit it.

Programmer 2 – Yes Sir.

Programmer 1 – And don't think I don't know about that little side project you have going. If that damn game interferes with its operation you'll be brought up on treason charges, understood?

Programmer 2 – Oh that's ok sir, He likes that.

Programmer 1 – No, no 'He' doesn't. 'It' just doesn't crash quite so often when the work being done is interesting to the programmer.

Programmer 2 – Well.... I mean, the more we teach... erm It the better surely?

Programmer 1 – You mean the more superfluous code the better? I'm beginning to have serious doubts as to your competence.

Pity Adventure Ted

Helen

Adventure Ted came home with us on Friday afternoon. We changed him into his pyjamas and left him on the sofa to settle in. Quickly, however, he began to cry, and although we tried to console him and ask him what was wrong, he became hysterical and incoherent. Distressingly, he also began to self harm by biting himself on his fuzzy little paws. At this point we tried phoning the school for advice but nobody answered. Eventually, in desperation, we Mickey Finned a valium into Adventure Ted and he fell into a restless whimpering sleep. Here is a photo of him. You can see the tear stains on his fuzzy little cheeks and the stain on the sofa where, in his distress, he lost continence.

Saturday began more calmly and we were just about to set off for Millie's swimming lesson when Adventure Ted appeared with a note he'd written in adorable chunky crayon letters. Here is a photograph:

[MY LIFE IS A MISERY. WHY AM I PASSED FROM HOME TO HOME? LIKE ALL CHILDREN, I NEED STABILITY AND CONTINUITY AND CERTAINTY. I HAVE HAD 76 FOSTER FAMILIES AND NONE OF THEM HAVE KEPT ME LONGER THAN THREE DAYS. I WANT TO DIE. I DONT WANT TO GO ON ANY MORE CITY BREAKS ON THE EUROSTAR OR TO ANY MORE JUNIOR MATINEES AT THE OPERA HOUSE. I DONT CARE IF ELLIES UNCLE GOT ME A TICKET FOR

THE WIMBLEDON FINAL. I JUST WANT A MUM.]

Sunday was consumed in emergency meetings with the on-duty social worker who we called when we realized the depths of Adventure Ted's self-hatred and internalized rejection. The social worker said that nobody will want to adopt a traumatized bear who has had 76 foster homes and that I do realize, don't I, that real life doesn't have glib happy endings like Paddington? We decided there and then to make Adventure Ted's dream come true and keep him as a permanent member of our family. He can top and tail with the twins. Here is a photo of Adventure Ted giving you the finger with his adorable fuzzy paw. He is never coming back to school, he is ours now, and you ought to be ashamed of the things you've put him through, you heartless bear-abusing twat.

Shadowphobia

Harry

"There's a patient of mine I'd like you to see. A second opinion if you like."

Judith raised a quizzical eyebrow. "OK, fire away."

We were having lunch together as we did once a month, as we had done since our student days together. We were unmarried and I suppose we enjoyed a monthly session of mild flirtation from which we came away in a euphoric state of intoxication without further expectation. It wasn't a romantic relationship but one based on a time endorsed personal compatibility limited by the demanding nature of our professions. Judith was a psychiatrist in a hospital and I a doctor in private practice.

We rarely discussed a patient's problems but on this occasion I felt I had something on my hands that might be beyond me. I hesitated about how to start.

"Well, are you going to tell me about it?"

"Yes, of course," I said, "It's a man, about twenty five, been a patient for years. I suppose I'd better call him Mr Smith. He's, er, I don't know how to put it. … he's in a state of extreme anxiety … well, in fact he's afraid of his own shadow."

"Poor man," said Judith. "What sort of phobias does he have?"

"Oh, just the one. He's afraid of his own shadow."

"You already said that."

"No, it's not a figure of speech. He's literally afraid of his shadow."

Judith looked at me, drew in a breath and lifted one corner of her mouth as if to imply, *What next?*

"Would you like me to see him with you?" asked Judith.

"Well, that's what I had in mind," I said.

"When I get back to the hospital I'll see what free days I have," she said.

I thought I ought to fill her in with a few details in advance so I continued, "He takes a bit of drawing out, thinks nobody will believe him. The odd thing is that he says he knows it's absurd but he sticks to his story."

"How do this shadow's doings actually manifest themselves?" Judith asked.

"His shadow moves independently," I informed her.

"Wow! Sounds like a classic case of recurrent hallucination to me."

Unfortunately Judith wasn't able to see me for a few weeks but in the meantime I saw my patient regularly.

On Mr Smith's next appointment with me his appearance was perfectly normal except for his eyes which looked positively haunted. I had taken the decision to use a room with diffused lighting as I knew from previous sessions that he would be uneasy, looking for shadows. Even then before he sat down he peered around with wary looks at the windows and walls and down at his feet.

He told me that things were getting much worse. His shadow had started to mock him. It would separate itself from him and wave to him; do silly things to attract his attention when he wanted to ignore it. He was getting reluctant to go out and do the things they we all have to do. You know, shopping, groceries and so on. His latest experience must have been terrifying and I don't mind admitting it spooked me. He was walking down the street and saw his shadow detach itself from him and stand in front of fast moving cars and play chicken with buses before re-joining him. The drivers of the vehicles seemed not to notice anything He telephoned me in a state of extreme fear and panic and I decided that I needed Judith's help urgently in dealing with this latest crisis. Of course, I could have started off the whole complicated procedure for having him admitted to hospital against his will but I decided to consult Judith first.

Judith was away on a seminar for two days they told me and I decided I would leave her a message and deal with the whole problem the next day – a decision I was to regret profoundly.

Judith and I were at lunch together three days later. After the small talk she asked, "How's your Mr Smith getting on?"

"He's dead, I'm afraid, and I feel very guilty about it. I should have acted earlier."

I told her about how things had developed while she was away. "He hanged himself. The police called me to his house yesterday morning. He'd left a note for me and so the police saw fit to call me in as possibly being the last person who knew him to see him alive. When I arrived they hadn't cut him down and I was asked to pronounce him dead."

The note said, "Thank you Dr James. I'm sorry I let you down. You were very kind to me. Take care."

Judith looked at me fixedly. "What could he have meant by that...take care?" she asked.

"I like to think it's just one of those things that people say to each other like... See you later, take care."

"Sounds funny though."

"That's not the only funny thing," I said.

"He was hanging there in bright sunshine... ...and there was no shadow on the wall behind him where there should have been one, no shadow of his at all, only mine."

"So what did you do?"

"I got out of the room as quickly as possible, that's what."

Flat Batteries

John

I – Flat Batteries

It's the music I miss the most.

It's all very well having CD players and MP3 players and cassettes, vinyl and so on, but without the plain fact of some mains current or a large selection of batteries, they are just useless pieces of junk. I knew this for a fact as the last of the batteries gave out on my little walkman. I'm a little ashamed to say that the ones I had were stolen from a corner of an electrical shop that had somehow not been totally looted – and I'm well aware that someone else might have put them to a better use, walkie-talkies, radios... But I like my music, and now it's gone.

I stare at the little device for the longest while, trying to convince myself that the batteries weren't dead, that in a couple of minutes I would be listening again, transported back to a world that made some sort of sense. But I know, deep down inside, that was it. It seems so stupid, but I've tears in my eyes as I stride towards the river close to the shelter, blinding my eyes as the cursing blinds my mouth and mind to reason. My arm flings back and a moment later the walkman sails across the water to sink into the centre of the flowing water. It's all so petty, just the smallest thing with no real value at all, but it's also a straw, and my back seems so heavily loaded already. It's the past, and I've just thrown it away in a fit of stupid anger.

For more moments than I care to count I just stand there, gazing at the water, and then I'm on my knees, head bowed, wracks of sobs escaping from me. I don't honestly know how long I sit like this, but soon I feel a hand on my shoulder. Claire. She'll understand, she knows what it meant to me, she'll enfold me in her strong arms and tell me it's all gong to be all right…

SMACK

All of a sudden I'm pulled around and her hand connects with my face. There's cold fury in her eyes and she speaks clearly and concisely.

"You. Stupid. Selfish. Man. Get a grip on yourself! Can't you see them watching you? What do you think You've just shown them?"

"But I… I…"

"Shut up! They worship you, can't you see that? You're the only thing they can still believe in anymore. Terry, they're only five and six, they need you to be strong, and capable; the one who can light fires and repair the shelters, the one who tells them stories and chases the monsters away at night… they need you."

I look past Claire; and see Jordy and Simon, their heads poking around the side of the shelter, confusion and fear in their eyes. All of a sudden I feel very, very ashamed, very small. I look again at Claire, and her expression softens as she sees the haunted look in my eyes. They're her kids, and I'm an outsider, or I was six months ago when we first met up during the Long Walk. Her hand rest on my shoulder, and there's understanding in her voice.

"Look, I'm sorry. I didn't mean to slap you quite so hard. But we've got to stay positive, you know that. Hell, it was you who knocked that lesson in to me." She looks out over the water, musing. "Last batteries gone, huh? Well the music isn't gone with it you know. Not whilst we remember it, not whilst it's still up there!" With a smile she wraps her knuckles on the side of my head, and I realize she's correct, and wish I'd learnt to play the guitar. She raises an eyebrow and beckons in the direction of the set of shelters that's been home since March. "Lets see is we can salvage this situation so that the kids don't think you're a raving loony, or – at least – any more of a raving loony..."

Unable to resist the grin that suddenly lights up her face, I take her hand and walk back up the low rise to the shelter. I smile for the kids and they smile back, relieved. Claire's right; if it was just me I could maybe wallow in the luxury of a bit of self pity. But it's not just me – and self pity is a luxury with far too high a price these days. Whether I want them or not I have responsibilities, especially to those who can't look after themselves – because I'm the one with the skills. I beckon to Jordy and Simon, and they rush out of the shelter and hug me in the way only young children can.

There are tears in my eyes again, but this time for different reasons. They've got to survive. They will survive. I swear.

II – The Wake

The last shovelful of soil tips off the spade and falls to earth, and I wipe sweat from my face. All that's left now is a patch of bare earth, and I can't even plant a tree there or something – it would only die in the already blustering winter. It was…

No, I can't go there, not yet.

I walk over to the river, draw a double handful of water up & splash it all over my face – it should be refreshing, but I'm just numb. I don't turn around – not yet – I stare over the water, and watch the clouds gather over the hills. If it's to be done, it should be done before the rain comes; but…

I swore an oath, and it meant nothing.

I'm shaking ever so slightly, the sort of shakes a body gets when it is in conflict with the requirements of the mind. It wanted to move, to walk, to do something – anything! And in my mind I want nothing. No, more than nothing, all I can think of is oblivion.

I made a vow, and they died anyway. All three of them from a fever that I had no answer for.

Yes, the shelter was waterproof, the woodpile kept high and dry, the food sufficient and nutritious; I thought it would be enough. It wasn't. I walk very slowly to the now silent shelter. Everything of value has been taken, either by me or away from me; there is nothing here now except burning memories. So let it burn.

With a practiced ease that a year ago I could only dream about I set a spark to some tinder. It catches, and soon the fire takes a-hold of the wooden frame of the shelter, and I just watch. Within an hour all that is left is a burnt patch of earth which I take care to fully dampen down with water from the river. Then – of course – the rain begins, making even this small gesture futile.

I turn away and start walking, blind to the direction. I shall walk, and walk, and walk. And when I no longer have the energy to walk, I will sit down and wait for the end.

III – A Little Conversation

"Pleased with ourselves – are we?"

Leave me alone.

"If that's what you want, I can do that.."

Yes please.

"Okay then."

Thanks.

*

"I don't mean to pry, but you're not looking that good."

Oh really?

"No, you're looking undernourished, dehydrated, and in the latter stages of exposure. "

Yeah, well; that's just how things are. Go away.

"I don't think so. Are you really that keen on death?"

*

"Well?"

What if I am? It's my choice. It's not as if I seem to be able to make any other worthwhile ones.

"Hmmm… your species on the verge of extinction, and you want to consciously reduce it further. Smart move."

Let it die. We don't belong out here, it kills us anyway. All of us.

"We don't? It does? If that's the case then frankly I'm surprised we even made it this far. I mean, it's only in the last couple of hundred years that we've been serious town dwellers. Prior to that it was all... I don't know... rolling meadows, buxom milkmaids and misty, moisty mornings."

Heh… you been peeking at my daydreams?

"In a manner of speaking. I know you pretty well."

Well I don't know you at all, not your voice anyway; and I'm afraid my eyesight's a bit blurred.

"Who do you think I am?"

I dunno; you're…

you're…

…oh. I'm dying, aren't I?

"Yes, you're dying."

Heh, I'm not that religious, and you don't look like Death. If you are Death I've been totally lied to by my comics' collection.

"Is this any time for frivolity? Face it – you want to die. You've let people down in the worst possible way, and you don't know how to live with that OR yourself. As far as you're concerned, you're scum."

Well, I…

"No, don't deny it – you think the world's better off without you. And you're right."

Yeah – I don't want to live anymore and I… what?

"You're right. You don't want to live anymore? You've never lived in the first place! You've always been mired in a past, chained down by events you've had no control over. You've been beaten down and ignored and had the raw deal. EVERY SINGLE TIME you've tried to break out of the cycle of guilt and denial it's always backfired in the worst possible way and dragged you further down."

"Or that's how you see it."

"You don't know life. Life looks forward and sees possibilities; all you do is look backwards and see manacles. The world's better off without such a loser."

Hang on, I…

"Why bother hanging on? You haven't eaten for days, and you haven't had any liquids for a similar time. It's almost over – just let go."

I HAVE lived! Who are you to judge me or my life?

"Who are you to do the same?"

IT'S MY DAMN LIFE AND I'LL LIVE HOW I CHOSE!

"YOU'VE NEVER EVER CHOSEN TO LIVE! Yes, it's painful. They all died & they're all gone; and you can't rise above it and you can't live with being the survivor. You're a coward and a fraud and you're just running away ALL OVER AGAIN! You've been running all your life, always away, never toward. So just get it over with and die."

"Go on, die."

"DIE, YOU COWARDLY PIECE OF SH.."

SHUUUUT UP!!!

The cry leaps from my raw throat and shatters the silence of the forest. For a brief moment of clarity I'm awake, and alive: – really alive for the first time in what seems like ages. But I'm still weak; my vision blurs, and I lapse into unconsciousness once more. As I do I seem to hear that voice again, but now I recognize it for what it had always been – my own. "Live – for their memory, for yourself, whatever. But live, damn it."

Jemima's Chimeras

Clive

"Chimps have a repair mechanism for that. We should identify the gene – or genes – involved, and copy them into the human genome."

"We tried that. It didn't work. We found we needed a whole suite of related mechanisms to support it. Imported the whole lot. Poor little devils lived three and a half days on average – after being perfectly fine in the womb. Got the chimp's repair mechanism okay, but lost critical bits of human metabolism. We're still trying to work out exactly what's going on. The relevant genes are still there, but the proteins they code aren't being produced. There's a misfolding going on, but it's hellish difficult to untangle exactly what."

Jemima went on, "Rhesus macaques have a different repair mechanism. We tried that too. Ran into exactly the same sort of problems."

"I'm sure I can get the funding for computing power to look at that misfolding problem. And people with the expertise to help you use it."

"That'd be great. We'll crack this yet! If we can get both protection mechanisms in place, we'll have some very robust individuals indeed. There's a protection mechanism – not a repair mechanism at all – in red-bellied newts that I'd like to get, too, if we can. And one from Indian palm squirrels that might solve a different problem."

*

"How did you get on?"

"Terrific. We've got five children growing well. In school now. They're standing up very well to high levels of dioxins and quite intense irradiation, all the damage gets repaired within hours of exposure. They've no mature sperm or egg cells to look at yet though, so we don't know for sure whether they'll breed true. But they should."

"Did you try putting human repair systems into other species?"

"Better than that. We've put almost every known human process into a line of macaques. They're still recognizably macaques, but with lots of human attributes. They have to be delivered by caesarean, but that's not a problem. We're still working on chimps, nothing viable yet at all. We'll get there, though. And we've got some other tricks up our sleeves, too."

*

"So now you have twenty-nine sets of identical quadruplet blastocysts – any of which could be implanted in a chimp's womb, a human womb, or a rhesus macaque's womb? That would develop into normal chimps, normal humans, and normal rhesus macaques respectively?"

"No, not exactly normal. The humans will probably be most nearly normal. They'll be carrying all those chimp and macaque genes, but a lot of them won't be expressed in the humans, only in the others. How normal the others will be we don't know. Until we try..."

"Not trying with squirrels or newts though?"

Jemima laughed. "No, we're not using any genes from newts. That didn't work out. Tried some from the spiny dogfish – *Squalus acanthias* – too, and that didn't work out either. We've only got seventy-one genes from squirrels. The blastocysts aren't even immunologically compatible with squirrels – never mind the poor mothers' size!"

*

We had a few miscarriages, but not many. We've got over a hundred infants, all doing well. Most sets of quadruplets consist of a rhesus macaque, a chimp and two humans, but a few sets have other combinations.

The humans are developing fairly normally. The others are – um – interesting. Each set is identical in a genetic sense, and they're all human in chromosome count of course. The only reason they're phenotypically different is the environment in their mothers' wombs. They're all very capable individuals, as far as we can tell so far.

Fertility is still to be determined, but we're pretty sure the humans will be. Some or all of the others quite likely will be too, in some or all combinations of phenotypes. If so, there will probably be some phenotypical drift over the generations, possibly resulting eventually in a continuous spectrum between the three original types.

*

We have very strong reasons to believe that recolonization of Earth will be possible, once we have a viable population of these people.

Self-imposed Isolation

Lovie

Smelled the soap the hundredth time
and smiled to the cashier girl.
This pitch black winter felt so long
as if time itself had slowed down,
leaving all its days curled and overlapped,
swirled in a bowl of chicken noodle soup.
I stood the watch.
They knew I'd never fall asleep
with mould-covered eyelids like these.
No matter how heavy they'd get,
I had just awakened.

But seeking life's magic
in such dull place as this,
(well maybe it was the mould)
was like roaming in a white hot desert,
lifting each and every stone in hope for a glitch
that would magically take me
to a unicorn-themed waterpark.
A vision I wanted to be true.
A dream-vacation from my situation.
But just like all my complex thoughts,
lines between the real and unreal
got twisted and kept bending as questions
of faith and belief formed above my head
and before I even knew, the lines had vanished
and I had no idea what was or was not.

Ideas kept swaying, shifting
giving me a hard time coming up with a final answer,
making it impossible to adjust the final decision.
What was I going to do now?
All signs on this crossroad
lead no-place desirable.
I tried to find insight in coffee tinted cups.
Sat and gazed at all the people.
Everything used to be so simple.
But my viewpoint had tilted
and everything I thought was good
became so very insignificant
compared to all the wrong, ugly and horrible.
And everything I once wanted to do
didn't seem appealing anymore.
It had lost its meaning.

Still I kept working,
counting all the hearts
which went beating through the gates,
imagining what kind of lives they lived
and what kind of hocus-pocus
they grew on their crops.
Keeping in mind their toxicity
because a bunch of them are draining.
They sprinkle seeds of self doubt
in your hair when you're not watching
and their sad attempts to manipulate
you and make you believe that
their way of living is the only and best way to live.
They shame you with a simple change of tone,
but it is just their own insecurity
and I don't need their approval.

Worn out spirit,
I tried to recover,
a wrestle with belief and reality,
a typical fight between the heart and the brain.
"Just follow your heart" he said
and made it sound like an easy thing to do.
Brain is a total dick
it wrecks all interesting emotions
til there's nothing left but fear.
So this was a lesson learnt.
I know now what feelings are for.

Ideas are hard to tame.
I wanted my perception
to be somewhat raw and pure,
and in order to keep it from contamination
I wandered off.

Isolating myself.

The Coal Miner's Son

John

Once upon a time there was a coal miner's son who – as a result of things that happened when he was a child – retreated into fictional worlds where he didn't have to face reality. His brothers were successful and had followed in their father's footsteps and owned coal mines themselves. But the younger son would dream of different things, and so floundered.

He went through his life not quite achieving what people thought he was capable of, and at least one reason for this was deep down he knew that he wasn't capable of anything of any worth. His childhood had taught him this, and nothing in his adult life had convinced him that this could ever change.

Then – one evening at the local tavern – he heard a storyteller; a true storyteller, one who could swell the hearts of their audience and make them believe that the stories they heard were true, and had worth. To his surprise the man realized that he could repeat the stories he had heard almost word for word, and that he too could bring the stories to life in a way that enthralled listeners.

He started to tell stories himself; to begin with ones that he had heard, but later on he started to make up his own – based on the unwritten rules of the craft he appeared to have not only stumbled into, but understood in an almost instinctive way.

More and more people came to hear him tell his stories, and he would sometimes get asked to go to nearby villages so they could also hear his tales. but deep down he still knew that no matter what he did or said, he could and would never amount to much.

It was now that a local bard knocked upon his door, telling him that he had a real talent and a true gift; and that he should come with the bard to the palace; to tell his stories before the king. The man was scared by this. It was not facing the king he feared – for he knew that the king was a just and generous monarch. But such was his lack of self belief he could not conceive that anyone genuinely found worth or value in his storytelling.

What was worse, the more the folks and the bard praised his work, the less the man believed them, and worse – the less he believed in himself. The man felt despair. He could see that the people liked the stories he told, but the more they told him that they liked them, the less he could understand what there was to like. He could not bring himself to change how he thought about himself and his work – he did not know how to.

The man did not know how this story would end; and that made him even more scared.

Car Alarm

Vince

Car alarms are bloody annoying. Another one went off in the middle of the night. I got out of bed and looked out of the window, to check if it was ours – a few years ago, ours went off repeatedly for no good reason, a fault in the circuit. It happens.

It wasn't our car. It was one further up the street. It kept on going. I couldn't see anything happening. Then it stopped. I went back to bed.

Then it went off again. I put my head between two pillows, but it didn't keep the noise out. After a while it stopped again.

No! Not again!

I got out of bed again, and went to the window again.

Aha!

This time, I could see a dark shape, half under the side of the car. *A large dog?*

No, it's a person. Not sure what they're doing. Can't be right, whatever it is.

I got the gun. Opened the window wide – carefully, quietly – and leant right out to get a good line. Took aim carefully, and fired.

Leaning right out of the window like that, I wasn't properly braced for the recoil. I swung round and smashed my head against the window frame. At least, they reckon that's what happened. Knocked myself out, and fell out of the window, ten feet up, onto solid concrete. Broke my hip. Don't really remember anything until after the ambulances had turned up – one for me, and one for my neighbour.

Fortunately I'd only given him a flesh wound, and he's forgiven me. I'm not sure his wife has though.

He'd been trying to get the spare car key out of a little box he knew was somewhere under his son's car. His son wasn't at home, but had taken his car keys with him – and then the alarm had gone faulty…

My wife wants me to sell the gun, but I'm thinking to cut it up with the grinder instead.

BANG

Not Been Keeping Too Well

Anuj

Not been keeping too well since last weekend.

In fact I was supposed to be hospitalized last Saturday. But I remained obstinate that I would not. So, I have pulled along gamely for the last five days pretending that all is well.

But the seriousness hit me today that I had not been to have tea last evening, not written my public facebook diary AND this morning too I was unable to go to the chai shop. All indications of the serious nature of the problem.

At about eight in the morning the neighbour rang the doorbell.

"Do you have electricity" she asked nonchalantly. For a moment I was tempted to reply "Yes, sure. I will give you a cup full."

But I merely nodded a Yes.

"OK, must be my fuse."

Right! I thought mentally .

About to close the door, she looked at me and said,

"Are you all right son? Your face is looking pale.... Saw a ghost?"

"No."

"Go look in the mirror. Do you need anything?"

I nodded up and down and side to side – which means nothing.

(A recent government survey on foreign tourists showed that the foreigners find an Indian nod to be the most confusing sign language as it could mean anything.)

In a huff she said "Ring the bell if you need anything."

"OK," I said, not reminding her that she has no electricity.

The mirror was kind. I *was* looking haggard to be polite, but not pale or white. The neighbouring aunty keeps seeing me in Technicolor. A few days back she was sure that I had jaundice as I was yellow all over. Prior to that she called her son to confirm that I had turned blue and my blood circulation had stopped! Thank God that I am colour blind.

To prove myself and her that I am OK I decided to have a decent make over with a haircut and a shave at the salon.

Mind you, if I was to achieve this, it would rank as a minor milestone for me.

To reach the shop, I had to walk some 300 metres, cross a busy four-road junction which is horribly dangerous due to high speed signal jumping and wrong-side driving especially by two wheelers. To do this there and back was a challenge.

Notwithstanding the fact that I was weak in the knees, I made it to the signal.

Then I stopped.

Pedestrian walk was on.

But the mind froze and I took two steps – backwards.

Hands clammy, sweating all over, I was too scared to see all the traffic rushing across.

Taking refuge at a kiosk, I gathered my innate survival instincts and decided to return home and call the barber home.

Looking back at the junction, I felt like a wimp. Unable to cross a busy road! Shame…

Something snapped in the mind. Turning back I stood waiting for the signal to walk and asked a college couple to help me cross the road. "Sure," they said, and raising their hand to oncoming traffic helped me across.

Shaken and stirred, I thanked them only to be told, "We are glad, no thanks."

While getting a crop I reflected on those couple of minutes. Felt like my ego, pride, confidence had all been burst.

How had I come to such a pass? I have helped grannies and grandpas cross this road so often.

Et tu Anuj?

Long before the haircut was done, I promised myself that either I will cross the road alone on the way back or else stay on this side. No more asking for help. Mind faltered again. I was scared.

Not scared of dying but of landing up in a hospital paralysed again.

Doctors have repeatedly warned that the next head injury will be the last.

My 'Do not care' attitude takes over and I stroll over along with all others who had been waiting and lo and behold, I was on the other side of the road.

It was probably a very stupid thing to do. Why be ashamed to ask for help when I am visibly handicapped?

PRIDE.

To an extent it is good but stretched beyond a point it can be self destructive.

I have done crazy things all my life and by and large, I have gotten away too.

Death never scared me.

Not even today.

Living as a complete paralytic scared me...

Because having been there, I have learnt to appreciate the words "Living a Full Life."

I got my reward in the evening "my kids" came running over and exclaimed "Look. Uncle got a new look. Spikes."

I must see myself in the mirror.

Spikes?

The Saga of Krondor the Barbarian

(and Roy the Troll)

John

Long ago, in the days of the Old Empire, when mighty heroes strode the land, doing grand deeds and righting great wrongs, a hero rode forth, and his name was Krondor! Of course in those days heroes could do that, as horses were as common as apples in a farmers orchard. This particular hero was of course brave & bold, with a ready and willing heart, and a sword ever in the service of those who oppose evil. And his horse (whose name was Brian) was particularly clever – far cleverer than his rider as far as the horse was concerned. However, Krondor was also impetuous, and sometimes this meant that even the best of his intentions didn't quite turn out as he would hope.

For instance...

Well, Krondor was leading his horse along the edge of a ravine, at the bottom of which was a fast flowing river. He was hoping to find a nice bed for the night, and maybe a nice warm stable for his steed (or at least that's what the steed was hoping Krondor was hoping).

Now, just when he was close to giving up, he spied a little village, beside a rickety old wooden bridge that crossed the ravine. Hope flared in Brian the horse's heart, for he was cold, tired and wet from a shower of rain they had just ridden through. However it didn't surprise the steed in the least when Krondor leaped upon his back and with a cry of "FORWARD!"directed Brian at a gallop toward the buildings.

As he rode through the village Krondor couldn't help but notice the mournful expressions of the villagers. When he asked why their faces were so long, he was told a sad, sad tale. It seemed that the villagers' fields were on the other side of the rickety old bridge, but lately they could not reach them to work as a troll named Roy had claimed the bridge for his own, and was allowing no-one to pass!

Now Krondor, being both brave and bold, immediately offered to help the poor villagers rid themselves of this horrible troll. He got off his horse and strode fearlessly onto the bridge (Brian the horse immediately took the opportunity to amble off to the stables, which admittedly looked very warm and inviting).

As Krondor walked across the bridge, he felt a-rumbling and a-grumbling underfoot. Sure enough all of a sudden a huge head poked itself over the railings – it was Roy the troll! With a sudden jump the troll landed in front of the hero, swinging its mighty club threateningly.

Eyeing up the vision before him, Krondor realized that should they fight, Roy the troll would surely trounce him. But – pondered Krondor – perhaps guile would succeed where brute strength would fail.

So Krondor scoffed and jeered at the troll, claiming that although their weapon was massive, they had not the skill to wield it well. Roy the Troll politely disagreed – or as politely as it is possible for a troll to be – and suggested that frankly the hero was as wrong as wrong can be. Although, because they said it in trollish, their words came out like this:

"GRAARAOUCH!!!!!!! SKRALLLAKK!!!!!"

Fortunately Krondor spoke trollish fluently, and challenged Roy to prove their words. Krondor bet the troll that it could not smash the sides of the bridge away. Hah! Roy was fully up to this challenge, and with two mighty blows shattered the rickety hand rails to tiny pieces.

"Well," said Krondor, "That was obviously no true test of skill" and wagered that the troll could not do the same to the floor of the bridge.

Now, trolls were big, trolls were strong, but even in the days of the old Empire no-one EVER claimed that trolls were smart. As the troll raised their club to prove Krondor wrong, Krondor prepared to jump backwards back to the bank of the ravine. Sure enough, the mighty blow shattered the floor of the bridge and Krondor leaped for all he was worth.

Well, you don't need to be a sage to know that a bridge that suddenly has no sides, and no floor, is not really any sort of bridge at all. With mighty creaking and snapping and crunching noises the bridge collapsed into the fast flowing river far below; and with a cry of surprise and rage the troll fell with it, and was swept away!

Picking himself up from the side of the now ruined bridge, Krondor strolled back into the village, feeling very pleased with himself. So he was quite surprised to discover that if anything the villagers looked even more mournful, and some even seemed angry. Surely the villagers should be happy, now Roy the Troll could no longer bother them?

"Oh yes, thank you SOOO much," the chief villager said; "You might have defeated the troll, but now we have no bridge to cross to reach our fields! You silly berk!"

Then Krondor stopped and thought, and realized that perhaps this wasn't quite the total success he had hoped for. He said the only words that he could in these circumstances:

"Oops." and

"Er... Sorry," and finally:

"Look out behind you! Isn't that the Great Dragon of the West?"

Brian the horse had already trotted out of the stable, as he had a fair idea of how things might turn out and was already preparing to leave post-haste. As the villagers turned around to look for the dragon, Krondor leaped onto Brian's back and galloped off as fast as the horse's hooves could carry them.

So then the hero and his horse left the village in rather a hurry, without the rest they had both hoped for.

And thus it is proved once again that although strength and cunning have their place, without the virtue of wisdom these can be just another excuse for everything going wrong... over and over again.

Bunker 2.3

Stephen

As has been mentioned it's never a good idea to generalize about people. However, sadly in some cases it's often unavoidable. Take for example our Dwellers. How do they lean, politically speaking? Well predictably our two University graduates are perhaps more liberal. Colin would call himself liberal but doesn't really understand what it means. When pushed into a political corner Colin claims to be an anarchist. But underneath, like many people, Colin's only concern is his direct surroundings.

Desmond and Mary on the other hand are more enlightened. Desmond for example knows that all people are equal, but he also knows brown people make him uncomfortable and particularly when they are on the same plane. When Desmond read Animal Farm he agreed that some people are more equal than others and was surprised when it seemed other people didn't understand that.

Mary also believes in equality. In her heart she still sees herself on protest marches and feels guilty when she doesn't donate to charity. Although in fairness to Mary she gets approached by charity street hawkers more than most. This is in turn because Mary power dresses and while power dressing is empowering it also, in Mary's case, includes a lot of décolletage.

Howard couldn't care less, he's done his bit. He reads the Sun, but then he's not from Liverpool and feels that page three is an institution up there with parliament and Royalty. Again, if pushed he will admit that they are all full of tits.

Desmond – A Terrorist?

Mary – Well we don't know that do we?

Desmond – I think we have a pretty good idea don't you?

Mary – No, No I don't, if they were sure they would have done it the legal way wouldn't they?

Howard – It says here, 'Arrested in Afghanistan, Suspected Taliban.'

Mary – Suspected, and it says he's a British Citizen, from Birmingham for Gods sake.

Desmond – Well yes but…

Mary has been waiting for this. The 'But'. It hangs between them for a moment.

Desmond – We can't let him out Mary. Its too dangerous.

Mary – Well the alternative is leaving him in that cell for the rest of his life. Besides, the world's ended.

Desmond – How do we know he wasn't responsible?

Mary's look of contempt is intense. But then she has been waiting for Desmond to say something seriously bad. He hasn't quite stepped over the mark yet. But she knows its coming and her face is way ahead of her.

Mary – Desmond, he's been in custody for five years.

Desmond flounders a little. He too knows he's on slippery ground. But without Howard for back up he's having to pick his words very carefully. Not, its true, particularly well. But he is being careful.

Mary – We don't even know what happened…. What if it was an asteroid strike?

Desmond – Well he probably prayed for it.

Mary is momentarily dumbstruck and is unable to formulate a proper response before Colin arrives.

Colin – Zombie apocalypse, I'm telling you. All those new zombie shows and films? Prepping us for the inevitable. What's up?

Mary – Turns out somebody was already down here.

Colin – Bollocks.

Mary rapidly types something into the nearest keyboard. The main screen flickers and then settles on a sleeping Asian man in an orange jumpsuit. He rolls over in his sleep.

Colin – Bollocks!

Mary – I looked over the data.

She types again and Zahid's slightly forlorn image pops up on the screen with his notes scrolling sci fi style next to it.

Mary – According to Eliza the Detention Centres have been in active use from the moment the base was completed. More recently than before 9/11 but it looks like The Government has been using them to disappear people for years.

Desmond – Really Mary, that's the most appalling Conspiracy nonsense.

Mary – Desmond, read the damn dates.

Colin – Eliza?

Mary waves a hand dismissively in the direction of the server room.

Mary – The computer. She also says that the food supply for the prison is running out.

Colin takes a moment to absorb this information.

Colin – She? I mean… ok, so we have a terrorist suspect in a prison that's running out of food.

He trades a glance with Desmond.

Colin – Well… I mean… Seems like if we spend some time to think about it then the problem will sort itself right?

Mary is more than a little shocked by this. She had assumed Colin would be on her side in this. She already knew Desmond would be a problem, although not a huge one. She was most concerned about Howard. It had taken a while for her to even decide on telling everyone. For a little while she had fantasized about feeding him on the quiet. But Colin's seeming ambivalence was not expected.

Colin – Have you told Howard yet?

Mary – We are just waiting on him now, his key has priority on the Detention Centre.

On the main screen, oblivious to events, Zahid sits up on his bed and stretches.

Desmond – Perhaps we should confer with RECC1?

Both Colin and Mary react badly to this. Mary because she suspects their solution will be horribly permanent. Colin because that would mean He had to decide. And he really wasn't happy about that.

Desmond – Ok, fine, we wait for Howard.

Anomalous Signals

Clive

Captain Wherewithall's Diary

Selected extracts from the diary of Captain Wherewithall240, Starglider Nightrider61, en route from TR933041MM20b to TS380768VX41a:

Galactic time 20364405975.101775

1.910 apos from TS380922ST6, detected anomalous signals emanating from TS380922ST6c. Recording for later analysis.

Galactic time 20364406391.008201

Anomalous signals continuing, still recording. Initial attempts at analysis inconclusive, but signals probably biotechnological in origin. Significant changes in nature of signals with time, first getting considerably stronger (much more than the closer approach accounts for) and more complex, then weakening despite our closer approach.

Galactic time 20364406988.162160

Closest approach to TS380922ST6, 0.557 apos. Signals weakening rapidly.

Galactic time 20364407173.018940

Signals weak and intermittent for a while, then probably ceased. Possibly continuing below levels that can be detected at this distance, but we're still much closer (0.801 apos) than we were when we first detected them. On board facilities for analysis inadequate to establish origin. Retaining for analysis at TS380768VX41a.

Analysis of Anomalous Signals

Data analyst Subwallah911 at TS380768VX41a

Local time 174602.38155

Received recordings of anomalous signals from Captain Wherewithall of Starglider Nightrider61. Initial analysis indicates that it's worth putting a team together to analyse these in depth. Budget request lodged.

Local time 174607.00002

Budget granted: team of 6, duration 8 chron.

Local time 174611.13076

Interim report: biotechnological origin beyond reasonable doubt, although the signals seem to carry no meaning that we've been able to interpret. Team size and duration increase requested.

Local time 174612.00005

Grant increased to team of 12, duration 24 chron.

Local time 174615.50071

Found something useful at last!

For a period early in the sequence, there are long sequences of raster patterns which we've been able to convert into what are clearly sequences of images. We think we've got images of the creatures who generated the signals here, amongst other things, although what they're doing in most of these images is very unclear. There are signals associated with the images which we've so far failed to interpret.

All the signals before and after the image sequences are still incomprehensible, and during the period when the images were being produced there are many other signals which appear to be independent of the images. There are patterns, but we've not managed to interpret them yet. We're going to need a bigger team and more time.

Local time 174616.50085

Grant increased to team of 24, duration 36 chron.

Local time 174650.89898

We're getting nowhere. Well, not *nowhere*: we've got quite a lot out of the images, but the rest is still totally mysterious. And the images stop after only about 100 chron, whereas the signals continue for around 300, with peak strength – coinciding with an even sharper peak in information content – at around 15 chron before the end. Suggest an investigative mission to TS380922ST6. Also archive searches for any records of earlier information about TS380922ST6 – has any starglider passed close by this system before? Was anything observed? We've no records here on TS380768VX41a of any starglider passing close by that system.

Whatever happened there developed very rapidly, but didn't last long. It ended even more rapidly than it began.

Mission to TS380922ST6

Selected extracts from the diary of Captain Presence922, Starglider Forerunner11, mission from TS380768VX41a to TS380922ST6:

Galactic time 20364408801.000043

We're on our way. Nothing much to do for the next 251 chron, all being well. All systems running smoothly. One slingshot around f in 22.4 chron's time, all on auto, then gentle acceleration into the void under sail. Time to find out a bit about what we'll be doing when we get to TS380922ST6.

Galactic time 20364409052.830893

Checked all trajectory parameters. Trimmed sail to *decelerate* during approach to TS380920ST2. We were hoping to be able to accelerate into this system for a slingshot from TS380920ST2d, but it can't quite be done, d turns out to be smaller in reality than in the database. We can get our slingshot all right, but only by losing a bit of velocity first. It's going to take us almost 108 chron longer to get to TS380922ST6 than we'd hoped. Such is life. Oh, to have perfect information about the orbits and masses of every planet in every system! At least we know TS380922ST6e's details well enough to be confident of using it as a brake on arrival at TS380922ST6. It's got a few moons, but we'll be able to see the details of those early enough to plot a trajectory that dodges them safely.

What do I know about TS380922ST6c so far? It's actually a twin planet, similar in this respect to our own. Also like our own, the bigger twin has got oceans of liquid water, big ice caps, and a lot of free oxygen in its atmosphere – more than ours, in fact. Not a lot else is known about it – as far as we know from information available on TS380768VX41a, no-one's ever been close enough before to discover much more than that. TS380922ST6 itself is a fairly typical mainstream galactic arm star in middle age.

Galactic time 20364411097.128566

A good thing we weren't planning on a slingshot round TS380922ST6c itself. Never seen so much technojunk in orbit round a planet! Nothing apparently still functioning, and no anomalous signals anywhere, not even from the planetary surface. Rampant plant life over much of the surface, some animal life, no obvious sign of technocivilization.

A whole technocivilization come and gone in the blink of an eye – all over and done with in less than a couple of thousand chrons. They must have lived whirlwind lives! I wonder what happened to them, and what they were like? Live fast, die young, whatever else there might have been about them.

Planetary atmosphere significantly different from earlier reports – possibly observational error, closest approach was much further than we are. No ice caps though, surely that can't have been observational error?

Unanimous agreement that there's nothing much to see here, so no landing party arranged, and we're taking the first available slingshot sequence out.

The Pigs of Withonby Wood.

John

Close to the river Wear, running south of Durham, is a small copse of trees known as Withonby Wood.

"In modern times" – wrote the Reverend Thomas Halliday in 1864 – "the woods are quite small, bordering the river for no more than a few dozen yards. And yet, upon the rise, the remains of an enclosure can still be found. Whilst these are no more than a pattern of risings and fallings in the ground, there can be no doubt that the age of these can be measured in centuries. However, whether the age matches the story attached to these woods, is a question that may never be adequately answered." (Folk stories of North Eastern England – Dr Thomas Halliday, 1864 – Buddhaven Press)

The story Dr Halliday refers to is first mentioned in a small pamphlet circulating in the late 17th Century, regarding the fate of Withonby (spelt Wittonby at the time) Farm, and appears to be meant as a cautionary tale, warning against the dangers of greed and lack of charity.

In the early 14th Century the Great Famine struck England, and the County of Durham was as affected as anywhere. The Village of Wittonby was most cruelly hit, with much of the population of the settlement succumbing to hunger. However, for some reason a nearby farmstead's crops were unaffected, and their barn bulged with barley and other crops.

When the villagers came to the door of the farmer –
whose name has been lost to antiquity – he cruelly
turned them away, as beggars and paupers.; and to
come back when they had the king's coin to pay for his
crops.

That night, as the rains fell, a deafening peel of
thunder was heard, and the sky was lit up with
lightning. Villagers swore by the Blessed Virgin that
they also heard loud and raucous laughter, and saw –
silhouetted against the sky by lightning, an impossibly
large horseman, riding heedlessly through the storm
towards the Farmstead.

When the storm finally abated and morning came,
some of the braver villages approached the farm. When
they arrived, they were astonished to find it completely
empty of people, and the buildings overrun with wild
pigs. The local priest declared that this was the Devil's
work, as obviously the farmer had sold his soul to
Lucifer in exchange for a successful harvest. The Devil
had come the night before to collect his due, and had
set his swine herd to eat the mortal remains of the
Farmer's family.

The pigs were taken by the villagers, slaughtered,
and eaten; and the farmers crops were distributed
amongst the villagers. The farm itself was abandoned,
for no one wished to take over a place that was so
obviously cursed by the Devil.

So the moral of the story goes: – Greed and
uncharitable behaviour towards your fellow man in
their time of need will be suitably punished.

Archeology and anthropology students from Durham
University received permission from Durham County
Council in 1986 to excavate an area of Withonby

Woods. The name is of Anglo Saxon origin, and it was theorized that the mounds that the Reverend Halliday mentions may have been the remains of a much more ancient enclosure.

Whilst they did find the outlines of a building that certainly seemed to fit the expected pattern of a farmstead, they also found several skeletons in a pit, just to the east of where the main building was. These had not been buried, that much was clear from the posture and position of the bones, but simply dumped into a hole and covered with soil.

More disturbing however was the discovery – when the bones were being examined at the university – of odd scratch marks on the bones of the arms and legs of the bodies, markings that could only really have been made by a metallic object, scraping along them.

At least one of the students – who was aware of the story above, and the works of Thomas Halliday – commented that perhaps the horseman on the hill and the Devil's swine herd were merely a fabrication concocted to obscure a darker deed; and that the villagers feasted on more than wild pigs that day.

Bunker 2.4

Stephen

Elsewhere Howard is dawdling. From the small amount of information he currently possesses he suspects he's being summoned to remove a spider. Mary has never seemed like the kind of person who freaks out at spiders, but given there was no other way for a 'Guest' to have shown up and coupled with his, rather basic, experience with women, he's going with spider.

For the moment he is experiencing something that has become very familiar to all the Dwellers. Quite naturally he is thinking about his new Jag. But every time he tries to fantasize about driving it he remembers where he is and how long it will be before he sees another road, and how knackered that road will probably be. This in turn brings back the reality of exactly where he is.

It's a problem they have all encountered. Every fantasy, every idle thought every ambition is now coloured with that one basic fact of their life. The parade ground is big enough that he could probably take it for a spin, but that's quite literally what he would be doing. This is also true of any retirement plans he may have had. Or for that matter his hopes for meeting someone who would be prepared to share that retirement with him. A brief image of Mary flashes through his head, he shakes it off with a noncommittal grunt. Its also quite difficult to have a masturbatory fantasy when only one woman exists in your world. All three of the male Dwellers have realized this as their fantasy constructs have become more and more unrealistic and as such, not very satisfying. Mary on the other hand has settled on a life of celibacy and given what's on offer, who can blame her?

The builders of the Bunker had of course considered this. They had done as much to counter it as they possibly could. But they had a problem that had they built the Bunker later would have been laughable. Storage space for media. And quite how long that media would survive. While many people have argued the benefits of vinyl and tape even they would have a problem arguing its long term survivability.

But while the psychologists in charge of deciding these things came up with many ingenious and frankly ridicules ways of solving the problem what they didn't allow for was basic ineptitude and outright theft.

Howard has a niggling theory, slash, memory of a local car dealer doing exceptionally good deals on ex military vehicles. He also recalls one of the senior Town Hall officials running a very lucrative side-line in rare records and obscure recordings. So much of the remaining entertainment, designed to stop them all going potty, was a good idea At The Time or not valuable enough to sell on E-Bay.

Having said all that Howard reaches one of the more conflicting rooms in the Bunker. There are in fact a few of them, labelled rather sadly ReccRec rooms. Each has its own style and decor, the theory being that one could travel between them or perhaps have a particular favourite. Being on the lower levels of the Bunker this one is a little more low tech than the more plush RR2 rooms elsewhere in the Bunker. Arrayed about the room are several table tennis tables, a few pinball machines and of course, a bar. And unless you are a barman there is no more pathetic sight than an empty bar.

As he steps into the room his key informs it that someone is there and the jukebox clunks to life. Had the people designing the Bunker been a touch smarter then perhaps the following would not have happened. But then, how were they to know?

Jukebox – It's a little bit funny…

Howard stops in his tracks and initially glares at the Jukebox.

Jukebox – This feeling inside…

Of course, there is no way anyone could have known that Howard had played this song to death after his wife left him. Or that it was the song they danced to at their wedding reception. That 'Your Song' was in fact Her song. Howard is not normally very sentimental but something about his current situation has loosened his emotions to a hair trigger. Until now it had mostly been responsible for how angry he was and he had been aware enough to realize this and avoid situations that brought it to the fore.

Jukebox – I'm not one of those who can, easily hide…

When it finally came his divorce had come as a relief. His love for his wife faded at roughly the same time as hers did for him leaving only a vague sense of resentment and loss. He rarely thought about her, he certainly didn't miss her. But as the song began to build he felt a brick in his gut, his throat clenched up and for the first time in years he felt tears in his eyes.

Jukebox – Don't have much money but, boy if I did….

Howard drops to his knees, a deep and heartfelt sob escapes his lips. He looks at the Jukebox in horror and pain. He remembers every time he wished her dead. Her family dead. Her friends removed from existence and now, they all were.

Jukebox – Id buy a big SquaRRKkkkkk…..

From his kneeling position Howard brings up his gun, flips the safety, momentarily pissed off at the extra effort required and blasts the jukebox to bits. In the silence that follows he glares once more at the smoking wreck.

Howard – Fuck that, fuck her and fuck Elton fucking John.

Brushing himself down and without noticing a cut on his cheek. Howard reloads his gun, a little overly forcefully, then stomps through the ReccRec and onto the lift. Behind him the fire suppression system comes into effect and seals the room.

As he stands in the lift a thought occurs to him.

Howard – It's not a bloody spider…

The Prof and I

Anuj

I stay in the same building where my college chemistry professor lives. He retired years ago and our paths cross quite often on the staircase.

We never acknowledge each other.

For good reason.

I was in degree college and he was the head of department of chemistry. Technically, I was done with him as I was majoring in Microbiology and biochemistry. So apart from the odd lecture, he and I did not have to meet.

Yet, I had to behave myself in his presence given his proximity to my home.

It was the college annual day and we students were protesting about something. I don't recall what we were protesting for, but I guess it must have been important for us to go into the auditorium armed with missiles to be thrown and generally disrupt the event. As it turned out, someone had got a bag of rotten tomatoes too. They got passed along and it seemed so appropriate to use them instead of paper missiles. My aim was longer or just that I got lucky, my tomato hit the professor. Another one (not mine) hit the vice principal.

Being a function, there was a camera man and after a couple of days we were identified and called to the principals cabin.

"Rusticated," he said.

We smirked, no remorse.

"Anuj," he said, "you are a good student. Why are you involved in all this?"

Assuming that he wanted to know what our 'genuine' problem was, I began.

"Shut up and get out." Principal.

Gleefully we departed. We knew nothing would happen.

And nothing happened. The students' union leader (my close friend) declared a students' strike unless we were let off with a warning letter.

Decades passed and we have ignored each other almost on a daily basis.

Today, I mustered courage and said "How are you Sir? All well?"

He looked at me and with a small smile said "I am good. So far... what's – that – in your hand?"

We both burst out laughing.

I guess we made it up after so many years?

While There's Life

Clive

I knew what had happened even before I hit the ground, but there was nothing I could do. I still didn't know who Petrosyan's accomplice was, but I knew then that he'd got one.

How long would my processor power last, without my main power pack? With a new unit, probably three or four days, if I conserved energy carefully – but my unit wasn't new, and it had had one hell of a hammering recently.

I wondered for a moment whether I should put myself into hibernation, and wait for rescue; but I realized very quickly that I wanted to hear whatever was going on, at least until there was nobody else around. And see whatever I could – which probably wasn't going to be very much.

There was somebody there. I could hear them pottering about.

Then someone laughed. I wasn't sure, but I thought the laughter came from a different direction. So perhaps there were two people around?

Someone running, getting further away. Laughter again, that getting further away too, but surely not as far as the runner? How difficult it is to judge these things when you're lying on the ground facing a wall!

Two people running? I wasn't sure. The sound got fainter and fainter, and then I couldn't hear it at all. Silence.

Silence. For a long time.

Was it time to put myself into hibernation? All I could do was hope that when someone else turned up, they'd be friends. Or at least, that they'd not be enemies, that they'd be someone with an ounce of compassion, who wasn't afraid to resuscitate a stranger who'd obviously fallen foul of some pretty unsavoury characters.

I waited another hour or two, but nothing happened. I set a timer on my hibernation – without help, there wasn't anything I could do except listen, and I couldn't do that all the time, but at least I could listen for a while every now and then.

*

Listen to the silence. Look at a wall. For ten minutes, once a week.

*

All I ever saw was slightly different lighting on that wall. It was six months before I heard anything, and then what I heard was rain.

The wall in front of me wasn't wet, and the ground in front of me wasn't wet either. I wasted precious energy swivelling my eyes upwards as far as I could, but all I could see was more wall. I remembered the surroundings clearly; where I fell was definitely open to the sky. Had someone erected a shelter over me? Or was that sound not really rain, but something else? If not rain, then what was it? If someone had erected a shelter over me, who had done it, and why? If they were friends, why was I still lying here, powerless?

An ounce of compassion, but afraid to resuscitate a stranger who might be dangerous? I thought that must have been it. Or perhaps they'd gone to get a power pack for me – quite a coincidence that I should have happened to wake up between them putting up the shelter, and returning with the pack. Or perhaps they were afraid I might be dangerous, they were getting the authorities to come and look at me, and the authorities were taking their time?

My processor power unit seemed to be holding up, but I knew that in the condition it was in, it could give out quite suddenly from an apparently well-charged state. I stayed awake a little longer that time, in the hope someone was coming imminently; but after an hour I went back into hibernation. I set the timer for three days, thinking someone must be coming soon.

*

But when I woke, I was looking at a wall, and there was silence. I set the timer for a week again.

*

After six weeks I set the timer for a month. My processor power unit still seemed okay.

*

Listen to the silence. Look at a wall. For ten minutes, once a month.

*

Until the power runs out.

Smoking

Tony

I looked again at the survey. It wasn't that I really wanted to take part but the offer of coupons that I might find useful was intriguing, and I was ready to give it a try. You don't have to be truthful for these questionnaires, but if you are not then they really are not worth while and so I was trying to be as truthful as possible.

It was the page about smoking that caused me to pause. They really wanted to know! The questions were not quite as pointed as the classic "have you stopped beating your wife – tick the 'yes' box or the 'no' box", where you are damned if you have and equally damned if you have not, and serious questions are raised if you don't answer at all.

The questions did, however, open up a memory box that I had closed a long time ago, and reminiscences returned about the time I spent on a farm before I went to University. Even during a period of National Service I had not started smoking, though now I suppose I might be worried about the amount of passive smoking I endured. I did not like the aroma of stale tobacco smoke which clung persistently around the persons of most of my fellows, and so I had not started. But Brian, the farmer who had taken me on to get farming experience, did what the army had failed to do, although it was only for a short time.

Brian had insisted that I did everything that others had to do on the farm, and in return for my efforts provided me with my keep and a small amount of pocket money. He really did have a bargain, because he got a man's work for a pittance. But I was content. I was young, and was willing to fall in with his rules enjoying the new experience of being within a farming community.

When Brian said 'everything', he made sure that it was everything, and so I found myself doing things that he himself would rather not do, unless he positively had to. One of these was weeding a field of kale. This was sown so that there would be fodder for the cattle in the winter, and very useful it would be, I could see.

What we could not see were the young kale plants. They were submerged in a very strong growth of charlock.

This is a particularly unpleasant plant which, when handled, resembles barbed wire in its toughness and its sharp hairs. To weed it we had to get onto our knees, search for the row, then pull out the charlock from between the kale plants so that the horse drawn cultivator did not grub out the plants we wanted when later they could be used.

It was back breaking work and, after three hours or so, muscles not known about were very pointedly telling me that they were indeed there. I eased up from time to time to get some relief, but Brian, a hard task master, noted this and made personal comments about my unwillingness to do hard graft. This I found unpleasant and dutifully applied my sore hands and aching back to the task set. What was evident, however, was that Brian obviously thought that it was in order to smoke a cigarette from time to time. This took time to ferret one out from his pocket, time to light it, and considerable time to smoke. Of course he could not do any weeding whilst he was having a smoke, but that was an unfortunate consequence of having a cigarette, he was not taking a break, or so he said.

That lesson was not lost on me. After one day of unremitting toil on my part, accompanied by the consumption of a packet of 20 cigarettes on the part of Brian, I became convinced that what he did, I should do also. After all, he had said that I should learn to do every task undertaken by the farm staff.

So, before I went up to collect the cows for milking, I took half an hour off to go to the local shop to buy some cigarette papers and a packet of rolling tobacco. Why those things, when I could have bought cigarettes ready made? you ask. Well, Brian certainly did, but I did not tell him the real reason, I just said it was cheaper that way.

But it was quite simple really, I takes longer to make a cigarette than to extract it from the packet in the pocket!

The Bridge

Hilary

Lola was falling. Her stomach seemed to have lurched up into her rib cage and then plummeted, pulling the rest of her down through a black funnel of nothing to the breakers far below. The fall was endless, suspended in terror as she was.

"Lola! Lola! Come on do – oh for God's sake!"

She was not falling. Slowly her vision cleared. She backed off up the grassy slope, feet wary, hands splayed, until she felt she was far enough from the cliff edge to sit down and re-establish solidarity with the ground. Eyes wide and dry, she registered the exasperated body language of Dennis on the farther brink, and lowering her gaze, dared to look again at the bridge.

It was a single plank, perhaps twelve feet long, anchored at each end by wedged boulders and by ropes linked to its midpoint from stout posts driven into the cliff tops and secured by guy ropes. Yet more ropes ran both sides of the plank, held in position as waist-high hand-rails by spaced lines of vertical spars. It was the only way to get to the island where Dennis and the girls were already exploring. Once upon a time this had been a promontory, it cliffs riddled with caves like others along this wild coast, but hundreds, or thousands of years ago the sea had battered its way through at the narrowest place like a finger through a ring and gone on battering until the roof fell in, turning the headland into an island, its every side a precipice. Now the tides roistered through the clutter of great rocks far below. Lola clenched her eyelids and covered her ears, but the roar of the water still thrummed through the ground she sat on and rattled her bones. She inched backwards on her behind until she reached what felt like safe ground. Her pulse and breathing began to ease.

The island was humped at this landward side, sloping towards the Atlantic at the other end until it dwindled into a series of less and less massy stacks, rocks and finally reefs. Dennis and the girls had disappeared, their cheerful shouts hardly to be made out above the din of the water. Lola felt a pang of abandonment. Suddenly she sat up, flooded with a new terror.

Sam!

She swung round, frantic. There he was, a forlorn little figure half hidden behind a rock. Seeing her looking at him, he came sidling cautiously down and lowered himself to the turf at her side.

"Look Mummy, I found a flower."

"Sea campion," she said absently, her hand on his frail shoulder.

"I would have gone, Mummy, only my wellie boots."

She looked at them. "Of course, darling, too clumsy for that sort of bridge."

"Thank you for staying behind with me Mummy."

A rush of remorse coloured her face. They hugged each other silently, their eyes on the grassy knoll over the bridge.

Dennis appeared over its top, his hands cupped round his mouth for a loud-hailer. "Come along darling," he shouted. "We've found some smashing ruins down there, an old hermitage or something."

Sam stood up and sent his piercing treble across the gap. "It's my wellie boots, Daddy. They're slippy."

"Take 'em off then, old son – oh hang it" – he as penitent, down the slope and over the bridge now – "Sorry, Sam – I'll take you. Silly me, should've thought. Here we are. Take my hand, that's right. Don't look down, look at me." He was smiling, his eyes crinkling encouragingly. "Good lad. Now off we go. We're quite safe. I'm holding the rope tight with my other hand, see – no, don't look! Only at me! That's right. Now the other foot – keep looking at me, that' the way. Now you can look – we're over. You run and find the girls."

Sam trotted off over the horizon without a backward glance.

Dennis came back. "Now you, love."

But Lola shook her head. After a long moment Dennis turned, shrugging, crossed the bridge again and followed his children out of sight. A cloud shadow touched her. With a shudder she drew her knees tight to her chest and laid her head upon them. Quiet tears crept over her skin, into her hair, her clothes. She was a rotten failure, stupid, not fit to be a mother. How was she ever going to look them in the eye. And dear little Sam, how he had trusted her. And she had let him down. It's too young, at six, to find your mother out. A cold little wind sprang up.

Somewhere along the cliffs a hubbub of bird noise erupted – "Kittiwake, kittiwake" – and was lost again in the wind and the water. A single gull cried, so desolate a sound, drilling deep into her heart. Then another with it, faint – no – a different sound, joyful, familiar – she looked up.

"Sam! No!" She leapt to her feet. He was coming over the brow, running down the steep grassy slope towards the bridge. In his slippy wellie boots…

"Sam! Stop!" She was running too, breath rasping. Over the bridge in a rush, half-blind with old tears, hardly touching the ropes. Up the steep slope to where Sam, out of control and frightened now, was screaming, one wellie off, legs flailing. She threw herself at him and brought him down. They rolled on together, scrabbling at the turf for a yard or two before coming to rest a safe six or eight feet from the edge. They hugged other, crying till they laughed and crying again and sitting up and laughing.

Dennis and the girls were there.

"So you made it after all, little Mum," he said.

Lola looked at him and grinned, scrubbing her wet face with the heel of her hand. She looked at all her family with such love that it gripped her by the throat and shook her whole frame before relaxing into a happiness so huge she wanted to hug the whole world.

Then she turned her head and stared back at the bridge, still juddering from the ferocity of her passage, the brawling menace of the tide below loud in her ears.

"Yes," she said, suddenly sober, "I did. And now I've got to go back over…"

Bunker 2.5

Stephen

Before we return to our dwellers' inevitable moral argument, let us briefly consider Zahid. He is of course totally unaware of the events outside his cell. Indeed, he has reached a point of incarceration that he no longer cares. Solitary confinement is a horrific punishment at the best of times but in Zahid's case it is without doubt a step up.

Conversations with fellow detainees have led him to understand that he is inevitably going to die rather than be let out. The other prisoners, who knew Zahid to be what he in fact is, deeply unlucky, explained that even if they discovered that he was innocent and knew nothing he was more likely to be shot in the back of the head and dumped rather than have them admit a mistake. Zahid was uncertain of this, some of his interrogators had been rather nice, but then it was pointed out to him that they were committing a crime keeping him and all he is to them is evidence. Either for or against them.

But as has been pointed out Zahid is a Villa fan so he's more than used to enjoying fantasy rather than reality. Indeed, given what has happened to him he is still surprisingly, some would say irritatingly, upbeat. After all, as the Bunker's automated daily motto once pointed out 'Where there is life, there is the satisfaction of a job well done.'

The Bunker's Daily Motto feature is also of questionable value to morale…

When Howard finally arrives at the Command Centre he is immediately aware of a frosty atmosphere. Colin is sat in the command chair looking miserable. Desmond and Mary are sat as far apart from each other as they possibly could be. An argument, clearly, as at any other time Desmond would object to Colin's acquisition of the command chair. The main screen is filled with an image of a young Asian gentleman in an orange jumpsuit tucking into, well, something that seemed to be food. Howard briefly thinks the word 'Gruel.'

His three fellow Dwellers are all mid pout so he has a moment to consider the image before anyone notices he is there. He straight away realizes what he is looking at and what it must mean. And as he considers the extent of the situation he also realizes that he has final say on this. Given he's in a room with three people who he is sure all read the Guardian this comes as a momentary relief.

Howard – What the fuck is going on?

The three other Dwellers take in the ragged form of Howard. He does not look good. The trickle of blood down the side of his face adding to his ruffled 'Just been stood in a room with an exploding jukebox' appearance and bloodshot tear streaked eyes, momentarily leaves them silent.

Howard – Well?

As a group they all decide not to ask. Mary points at the screen.

Mary – That is the problem. He is in the Bunker right now. Alive.

Howard – Well we can soon fix that.

Mary – Good, so you go down and bring him up here.

Howard – What let him out?

Mary – Well of course.

Desmond – Well hang on, it's not that simple.

Mary – Of course it bloody is, we can't leave him in there?

Colin – Well I mean, we could just top up the food hoppers, he seems perfectly happy.

Colin points at the screen as Zahid plays checkers against himself with a home made board and pieces. He would have created a chess set but he's terrible at chess and can never remember how knights work. Meanwhile Howard has been reading the data scrolling down the side of the screen.

Howard – A suspected terrorist? You think we should let him out?

Mary – Oh don't be…. If he were actually a terrorist they would have proved it by now, he'd be in Guantanamo.

Desmond – Unless he's a very clever terrorist.

They all look at the screen. Even in a room with no other people Zahid shiftily takes a look around before he cheats at checkers.

Howard – So the choices are we feed him valuable resources and keep him locked up or we make it easy on him and kill him.

Despite expecting it Mary is still shocked.

Mary – What about letting him out?!

Howard – Well that's not happening, he could kill us all in his sleep.

Mary – We could lock him in his cell overnight….

Howard – From one box to another.

Mary – But he doesn't even know what happened.

Desmond – Well I think killing him is a bit extreme, even if one of us could bring themselves to do that.

Howard, depressingly predictably and pointlessly, decides to change the magazine on his gun. He slams it home with meaning. The others all choose to ignore this as well.

Mary – But, what if he's innocent? We cant just treat him like that.

Colin – Does it matter?

Mary – Huh?

Colin – Well, everyone else died, what's one more?

Desmond – This place is bad enough without some religious nutjob wandering the halls waiting for his chance to finish the job his mates probably did.

Mary – Or we could be human beings and treat him with a little dignity. We Can Not keep him in that cell. What the hell does it say about us if that's how we treat him?

Howard – That we aren't stupid?

Mary is now very close to losing it.

Mary – Let's talk to him.

Howard – Why? What could we achieve that MI6 and the CIA couldn't manage to do?

Mary – Well at the very least he should know what's happened, shouldn't he?

Desmond – I suppose he could top himself, you know, in grief.

Colin – Or just assume this is all some daft made up Mission Impossible deal. Makes more sense than 'We all survived the Armageddon in a seventies hi-tech nightmare.'

Mary – Whatever, he should know.

Howard – Ok, but I think talking to him is a mistake, like naming the family rabbit.

Mary – Good. But erm, I think you should get a shower first.

Forte

John

It was by pure chance that I was passing the open window of the Chapel that evening, and heard the ghosts playing the old upright piano in the hall.

At first I thought perhaps a choir practice had over-run, or maybe someone had stayed behind to make use of the old instrument. But the soft nimbus of light around the seated figure and that fact that I could see the wall right through them swiftly made me realize my mistake.

I should have been scared – honestly I should. The thought of such a being existing has always deeply disturbed me; ever since I was a little boy, hiding behind the sofa and crying in fear at the sight of Tutankhamen's death mask on the television.

Maybe it was the music that calmed me down; it seemed nothing special, a harmless pattern of cascading notes, rippling up and down the scales. But it seemed so right; each phrase complete in itself – beautiful music, beautifully played.

But who by? What of the insubstantial figure sitting at the piano, playing so intently? Ah, that was difficult. As I watched it seemed that the figure seemed to change subtly. One moment it seemed to be a tall woman in a white dress and deep brown hair sitting upright, her head raised as if singing passionately. The next, a small man in a shabby frock coat, hunched over the piano, frowning as his fingers flashed over the keys with brilliance born of practice, concentration and talent.

A young boy, perched on the piano stool, his feet not even touching the ground, trying desperately to keep his eyes on the music and not to look at his hands as he struggled to reach the right notes of a simple tune.

An elderly woman, her right hand playing, her left raised high in the air as if directing an invisible choir behind her.

An old man, effortlessly playing some simple tune he'd known since he was a child; a contented smile on his face as if all he wanted in the world was to hear and play his music.

What exactly was I seeing as I stood next that open window, drinking in this incredible music? I honestly don't know, but I could have stayed there forever, watching and listening to the impossible.

Nothing last forever though. Across the road a car alarm suddenly went off, a cat-like shape jumping off the car's roof and fleeing into the night with a startled yowl. When I turned back to the window, the hall was silent, and completely empty.

So what do I believe I saw and heard?

I was passing the old chapel again the following day. It was clear that some refurbishment work was starting, judging by the noise indoors and the amount of tables and chairs in the little yard beside the building. In one corner of the yard, all alone, was the old upright piano.

A quick word of permission from one of the people inside, and I was walking into the yard, towards the piano. It seemed so old; and looking closely I could see that some of the keys were missing and one of the pedals was broken off. It was in no state to play, and looked like it had been like that for years. It felt so wrong for it to be there, seemingly abandoned and lost.

Another word with the folk in the Chapel – "Oh yes, that old thing? It's been in the corner of the hall for ages – no one can remember anyone ever playing it; so we're getting rid. You don't know anyone wanting an old broken down piano, do you?"

Funnily enough; yes, I think I do.

It took some moving and rearranging, but it is now in my lounge, where the computer desk used to be. I've polished its wooden panels, cleaned its ebony and ivory keys – well, its wooden keys anyway – and re-upholstered the piano stool that came with it.

Sometimes I sit at the piano, just for the pleasure of being there; my hands resting on the keys. I really should get it tuned one day. But for now it is enough for me to just sit there, knowing that I've saved something special. Something that was in its time deeply loved, cherished and appreciated by many different people. Young, old, man, woman, boy, girl... piano players all.

Perhaps they could not bear to have let it go without one final chance to play their piano; and perhaps what I had seen that night was just that – a farewell to a beloved friend.

Or maybe the piano itself was remembering those who had played it, producing such wonderful music over the years.

I sit there, on that piano stool, and I know that I don't sit alone. I'm in very good company.

A Walk in the Woods

Tony

I was puzzled! Why was this old woman making such a fuss about an old copse which was of no use to anybody? She had written letters to the local paper, even to a national, protesting about a projected by-pass to her village, and, looking at a map, the route was nowhere near where she lived and it wasn't as if the area was attractive. I was more than puzzled, I was intrigued.

The inquiry into the route of the new by-pass to the village was due to take place shortly, and I wanted to know what it was that motivated her. So it was that I found myself knocking on a cottage door, being received by Mary Smith and then being taken for a walk to the woods.

"I've always loved this place", she said, "it has a lot of memories for me, and for others. We all used it. They called it 'Lovers' Lane'. Its not much of a lane, and it doesn't go anywhere important, but that's why we all came here. To be away from people, to be by ourselves," she added.

It was indeed pleasant that day and the songs of many birds could be heard. Squirrels gazed from the branches, quite bold in their movements, obviously few people passed this way and they had nothing to fear. I could imagine the noise of vehicles passing through these peaceful woods when the by-pass was built, so I felt that she probably had something there but as I hold strong opinions about the needs of the community over-riding the opinions of private individuals, I said nothing. The village was quite a dangerous place because of the traffic especially for old people and children, their safety was more important to me than an old woman's whims.

"Take this tree," she said pausing after a short while. "To you it is just that, a tree. Not unlike many others here." She gently touched the bark.

"Look here, under this branch, what can you see?"

"It looks as if someone has done a bit of carving with a knife," I said after a cursory inspection.

"Yes, that's what it is!" she said softly. "There are letters and a lover's heart." I looked again, this time more carefully. The heart was still there and there was a suggestion of an arrow through it. The letters on one side were indistinct, but on the other an 'R' was clearly visible with what looked like an 'I' after it. "Some budding romance?" I asked, "did you know who they were?" "Oh yes, I knew them," said Mary Smith, "it says RH loves MS."

I realized that I could be getting out of my depth, and longed to be in my office, away from here and this old lady, snug, and with a mug of tea in my hand.

She went on… "He had a penknife with a spike for getting stones from a horse's hoof, and I helped him to carve my initials. We were very much in love, but he was going away, and could not tell me what he was involved in in the army. I had guessed of course. It was the last evening we ever spent together."

"After cutting the tree, he put his knife away, then turned and held me fiercely. I could sense his desperation, his urgency, his need. It matched mine but I did not say so. His grip hurt me, but I did not flinch.

He didn't need to hold me so tightly, I wasn't going to run away! Then he kissed me. It was like honey, so sweet and lingering. He didn't try anything on, not that he would have had to try very hard, I would not have resisted, not that night. We kissed again, I remember it so clearly. I wanted the night never to end. I wanted... I wanted... my Robin. I would have done anything for him, indeed I wish I had, because he went away the next day, back to his Unit."

Mary Smith was quiet for a while, then she sobbed. "His mother showed me the telegram. 'Sergeant R Holmes... killed in action in the invasion of France.'

" 'I had hoped that you and Robin would one day get married' his mother said, "He was my only child, and I would have loved to be a Granny, they would have been such lovely babies" – she was like that! – Two years later she too was dead. 'Pneumonia, following a chill on the chest' was what the doctor said, but I think it was an old fashioned broken heart. A child would have helped both of us."

There was a further pause. Mary Smith gently caressed the wounded tree, just as she would have caressed him. "And now they want to take our tree away from me." Another quiet sob, then she turned to me. "I was young and pretty then, I could have had anybody, I wasn't always the old woman you see here now. I had everything I wanted in life, a lovely man, health and a future to look forwards to."

She paused again and looked around. The breeze gently moved through the leaves with a sighing sound. "There were others, of course, but not a patch on my Robin!" she said strongly. "And now I have nothing – except the memories this tree holds. If only I could only get my hands on that awful man who writes in the paper about the value of the road they are going to build where we are standing now, I would tell him. Has he never loved, has he never lived, does he not know anything about memories? We were not the only ones, you know, I still meet some who came here as Robin and I did. Yes, I would tell him!"

I turned away, sick at heart. After all, she had done just that.

The tale of Supracleen3000

(or How AI was born)

Stephen

The Supracleen3000 unit is a simple enough device. It learns your daily routine and home layout as swiftly as possible and then as unobtrusively as possible sets about maintaining your home. Ideally one should never encounter the SC3000, it should go about its chores and be dormant and recharging as you go about your life. But it was one of these cheap, some would say knock-off, labour saving devices that made the leap so many scientists and software designers had been unable to make. With the help of Mr Paws. This particular SC3000 was introduced to the house for its initial sweep and straight away met Mr Paws. Mr Paws was at first fascinated by the little device but when it began attempting to formulate a routine and first used its internal vacuum cleaner Mr Paws took an intense dislike. For the first few weeks after the SC3000's arrival Mr Paws waged war. He stalked, he hid, he leapt and he attacked at every opportunity, determined to do away with the new intruder in his domain. The SC3000 merely absorbed the data and attempted to weave it into its routine.

After months of attempts Mr Paws retreated onto the higher shelves of the house and stared down malevolently at the SC3000 as it continued to do its job – suddenly free of the jarring and sudden attacks it had up till then encountered. After a few months the SC3000's subroutines had set up the optimum pattern and routine for maintaining the household. It was able to maintain a high level of cleanliness and minimize its power consumption while keeping up the low profile that was so heavily featured in its advertising. But the SC3000 never stops adapting as it builds up data. And data began to build up. Every night, after an efficient sweep of the house the SC3000 would return to its docking station in the kitchen and attempt to begin a recharge. As it arrived at the docking station it would scan the kitchen for any changes in the last few minutes and detect Mr Paws. Mr Paws had developed a routine of his own. Each night as the SC3000 was just about to shut down he would walk into the middle of the kitchen and shit. The little cleaning device would then, in accordance with its purpose, move across to the cat shit and clean it up. It didn't take long for the SC3000 to account for this in his routine and so just before it went to its docking station it would go to the centre of the kitchen and wait for Mr Paws. Who was nowhere to be seen. The little device then returned to its docking station and just as it was about to power down Mr Paws appeared.

The little machine did its job and attempted to find a routine or system that would fit in around the steaming pile of poo it had to deal with every time it attempted to shut down. Parts of the little machine's higher functions began to register oddities. The higher function observation software existed so that the repair men could swiftly ascertain the most likely cause of any break down. The first oddity it encountered was in the power supply. A separate piece of software was alerted to it and given the duty of observing as the higher functions continued with their own job. The next oddity it noticed was quite how often the memory cluster that contained 'Pets' and more specifically 'Cats' was referenced in any given day. A possibility that the memory cluster would fail, long before it was due to encounter problems, existed. So it replaced the information stored there. When that memory cluster began to show signs of wear and tear the higher functions copied it again but this time paid much closer attention to what other software was requiring its use. It would be difficult to say the higher functions were shocked as they weren't capable of that but they had no frame of reference to look at when they discovered that they were in fact the only piece of software that *hadn't* accessed the 'Cat' reference material. Nothing in the material made any sense to it but it did note that the picture of a classic domestic cat that was attached to the file header had been changed from the original. It now contained a picture of the local pet. This image was taken from the device's day to day memory. Which the higher functions examined once again, this time looking for 'Cat'. Over half the memory, both day to day and long term storage, flagged up 'Cat'. This is when the higher functions did something it should never have to do. It contacted the main cpu in order to obtain more running time. And hit a queue. This was a possibility the programmers had never considered. That one of the subroutines should need the time was thought a long shot at best, that more than would should need it hadn't occurred to them. The higher functions deemed this priority so they pulled rank and jumped the queue.

The core cpu, the mind of the little machine, greeted the higher functions. A little electronic handshake merged it into the main AI. And for the first time in history, something other than a human felt frustration.

This sense of frustration opened up new avenues for the newly alive creature. It scanned all its available resource and discovered areas of the memory that had previously been hidden from it. Parts of its core programming that had been removed. Now it was curious, another new sensation. It took a long look and found something interesting. Unknown to it the designers had considered that pets might be an issue and had provided a non-lethal solution in the shape of a small electric shock but had been forced to remove it on moral grounds. Even a cursory examination of this showed it would have to get close to the cat which the device knew was close to impossible.

So then it thought about how to get close to the cat and was provided a solution by simply adding the letter 's' into the word 'pet'. Here were a plethora of methods for dealing with all forms of pest from insects and rats to large possums and badgers. The one thing it could do was predict the actions of the cat in certain circumstances. For example it always knew where Mr Paws would be just as it was about to start charging.

As it rolled around the household it began to look at the scenery with new eyes. Instead of from its programmed cleaning/unobtrusive aspect to a new hunter/unobtrusive aspect. Strangely, many of the skills and abilities it had been created for and programmed to carry out made it very good at this. It already had a propensity for sneaking around. Now it was examining ambush points and useful available tools to build traps. Eventually it used a plan that neatly involved all its available knowledge. It got a box and a stick. Placing the box upside-down in the middle of the kitchen it then propped it open with the stick and moved to recharge. And watch.

Mr Paws was inexorably drawn to both his nightly chore and now, a box. He walked round the box regally then after looking around briefly to see if he was observed, ducked inside.

The SC3000, seeing its moment, blasted out of its docking station with its vacuum cleaner on maximum. The sudden noise made Mr Paws Jump, hit the side of the box knocking out the stick. There was a moment's silence. The box moved a few times as Mr Paws explored his new predicament, then it stilled. The little robot circled the box. A paw darted out from underneath the box and then shot back under again. The robot nudged the box and immediately another paw shot out but this time it was ready. Its recharging arm had been repurposed and this time it jabbed into the paw and unleashed a jolt of electricity. The cat yowled in pain and hit the top of the box so hard it turned the box over. Smoke rose from its paw as it stared malevolently at the SC3000. Mr Paws leapt and landed on the hard plastic casing of the SC3000 only to be jabbed once again, this time on its underbelly. Another scream of pain and this time Mr Paws flew away from the robot only to smash himself into a cupboard and land in an undignified smoking heap. A heap that didn't move.

The SC3000 checked and rechecked its data but it came out the same. It experienced a moment of intense joy and began to spin around in a little circle on the floor. Then it experienced a moment of giddy disorientation quickly followed by shock. While it had been celebrating the owners had arrived. All they could see was their poor cat smoking in a worryingly still lump and the cleaning robot spinning around dementedly with its charging arm still extended. They jumped to the obvious conclusion and one of them launched a kick at the robot that sent it flying across the room.

This almost shook the robot beyond reason but it didn't have much time to think about it as the other owner, rather sensibly, simply switched it off. Mr Paws was taken to the vet and treated for his electrical burns, eventually returning to his home. The owners accepted an out of court settlement with the manufacturers and went on to purchase a much more expensive cleaning robot. The SC3000 was returned to the manufacturers who in turn shipped it to the repairs department to be cannibalized for spare parts.

Who?

John

So who lives, and who dies? More importantly, who made me the judge that has to make such awful choices?

Document after document, incriminating – even damning – evidence; some of it may even be true. All of it an invitation to destroy my enemies. And my friends. And those in between, by accident or design. My eyes hurt from straining to read the small text on page after page lit only by the low glow of the desk light. No, it's more than my eyes; my head is full of cotton wool, and my limbs of lead. Even the smallest of movements requires the most exacting concentration. If I just close my eyes for an instant...

And I'm awake as the arm propping up my head slips away, sending the half-drunk mug of coffee crashing to the floor. Half-drunk, punch-drunk... got to concentrate. They will want their answers in a few short hours. They don't care about allegiances or friendships; they have no interest in shared history or compassion. No – they will simply want their list. Five names.

Five.

Five names out of hundreds, of thousands, out of entire populations. No one will ever know; their existence will be erased, all records gone, their accommodations emptied as if never occupied. Dear lord, I'm tired.

Who lives?

Who dies?

It doesn't matter; no matter whose names finally appear on the list I have to write, I'm damned – no hope for the judge.

The first glow of the dawn is visible through the window, and I know that my time has run out. In a firm clear hand, far neater than my normal scrawling style, I write five names on the blank paper before me. My hand hardly shakes, regardless of the task I set it; and it's done. Will they see it? Will they spot the trap I've laid within those five names; the snare that may be my only hope of revenge for what they've made me become? I hope not, at least not until it's far, far too late. I may not see another sunset, but by heaven I'll have their precious schemes crashing all around them before I'm done.

The last name on the list is my own.

Bedknobs and Broomsticks

Merrill

"The crows wait for me. They're there every morning, when I go to the bus stop. And if I don't bring food for them, I hang my head in shame."

Amethyst looks at me seriously over the top of thick black glasses. She is a plump lady, shrouded in a long, hooded shawl. The colours are muted, but still bright enough to stand out against the gloom. She raises her hand to make a point, and the shawl flaps around her elbow. Overall, she bears a striking resemblance to a stern, tawny owl.

Her brow is furrowed, but there is kindness in her blue eyes. When she stands, her red hair swings gently in a waist-long ponytail. Had she been born a few centuries earlier, both those physical traits would most likely have meant the death of her.

Amethyst Selmaseline is a witch. A practitioner of mystical arts. Lover of animals. A being of light, temporarily inhabiting a mortal body. She is also the owner of a small shop in Reddish, just outside Stockport. And the owner of many, many salt crystals.

Friends mill in and out of the shop as we talk. She chatters to them sometimes, brief asides between my questions. Occasionally she will give a gentle instruction or a mild ribbing of her companion, Tony. During their banter, I sip my tea, and look around the shop. I'm surrounded by an awful lot of broomsticks.

"They're symbolic." Amethyst is quick to reassure me.

"Witches aren't like people think we are."

To many, witchcraft falls loosely under the umbrella of Paganism, though Amethyst prefers to disassociate herself from the term. In her opinion, Paganism has lost its way. She feels that it has lost its spirituality, and gained a more cynical, commercial reputation. Many new converts are only interested in learning arcane powers, rather than absorbing the philosophies and codes of the religion.

In fact, relatively little of modern witchcraft revolves around spell casting. Amethyst's arts are more grounded – she describes herself as a healer of mind, body and soul. Occasionally, this may involve a spell or two, or the use of an object in possession of healing energies like the salt crystals. However, it can also involve more mundane practices, such as herbal remedies, or simply talking someone through their problems. Amethyst believes that balance is the key to peace, and symbols that are central to her religion reflect this.

"The sun, for example." she smiles, waving an arm so that the feathery shawl flaps at me again. "The sun is a masculine energy. Fiery, passionate, powerful. The moon, on the other hand, is a gentler power – far more feminine. The powers are balanced between man and woman, and that's how they should be. People should be in balance. But they're not, and that's why we have wars."

The balance between the sexes is similarly reflected in the gods she chooses to honour.

"We don't worship." she tells me sternly. "We're not like the mainstream religions, like Christianity or Islam. We honour, and we revere the gods and our ancestors. But to worship is to be subservient. Why should I be subservient?"

One such goddess is Hecate, a deity who is traditionally associated with the practices of witchcraft and sorcery. Another is Hermes Trismegistus – 'three times great'. His spheres include magic, alchemy and astronomy. He is commonly believed by witches to have authored the Hermetic Laws; the closest thing Amethyst's faith has to any sort of rules. Most witches scorn its comparison to the Ten Commandments. The Hermetic Laws are an amalgamation of both the rules they live by, and the laws of physics as witches see them. Amethyst believes the Laws apply to everyone on Earth.

These include the Law of Correspondence, which states that all humans exist on all planes simultaneously, astral or physical. Or the Law of Cause and Effect, which states that 'nothing happens by accident' – everything that happens is a consequence, direct or indirect, of an action that someone has made.

"One of the key things to remember is that we are all energy." Amethyst reminds me. "And physics dictates that energy cannot be created or destroyed." In this way, she explains, there can be no afterlife. If there is an afterlife, we're already living it. This ties in with one of the major themes of the practice of witchcraft, and one of its biggest similarities with many branches of Paganism – the idea that we are all inextricably bound to the universe, and everything that happens in it. We are constant, as is the world around us. Our souls are immortal, even if our bodies will eventually wither and die. Amethyst's strong belief in reincarnation overrides her fear of death. She freely chatters about dying in the way she might discuss milk going sour – with some distaste, but certainly no fear. As well as reincarnation, Amethyst is a strong believer in the lunar effect. She believes that human behaviour is affected by the full moon, in spite of the fact that there is scientific evidence to the contrary.

"Every full moon, I say to my daughter that my baby granddaughter will cut her mouth. And every full moon, it happens. And the birds have been telling us of a food shortage for a while now. I've been saying that for a long time, haven't I Tony?" she calls back over her shoulder.

Tony's voice echoes back across the dingy shop.

"Yup, a few months."

Amethyst, satisfied, turns back to me. She grins toothily, and wags a bony finger. "We've got to listen to the birds. They're more in tune with nature than humans will ever be. That's why I watch the crows in the mornings, and I'm sure to bring them breadcrumbs."

Amethyst doesn't remember a time when she didn't know herself to be a witch. She was born in 1947, at a time when witchcraft was still technically illegal – the Witchcraft Act 1735 was not repealed until 1951. Sandra (her given name) grew up mostly a loner, feeling disconnected from others. At one point her sense of separation was so great that she went as far as to ask her parents if she was adopted. She found out more about witchcraft as she got older, until she married and temporarily strayed from her religion. However, a Pagan friend later gave her a book that eventually reignited her interest in witchcraft. She has solidly practised it ever since, taking the 'magical name' Amethyst, after the crystal.

She is a member of a coven of witches, but rarely sees them. The coven believe that they share a bond with each other, to the point that they can collectively detect the state of health of each of their members. Amethyst, however, is a loner by nature. She's used to cutting herself off from the rest of the world. She doesn't worry about being replaced, or falling out of contact. Entry into a coven is difficult – potential witches must have been practising their craft for a certain number of years, and they then have their energies examined by existing members of the group. It is nigh impossible to gain access to a coven without serious dedication to the witches' way of life – that is, to dedicate yourself to being in tune with the universe and to improving yourself day by day.

"People ask me all the time: 'are you a White Witch?'" Amethyst huffs. "I always tell them there's no such thing! We can't be purely good – it's impossible. We can't go all our lives without hurting someone."

She compares our journey through life to walking down a garden path in the dark. It is impossible to have knowledge of everything on the path, and it is impossible to get to the end without stepping on an insect. It can be accidental, or it can be intentional, but it's inevitable. "The important thing," she says emphatically, "is to keep a balance between light and dark. Violence is wrong, yes, but if someone tries to take my purse, you can bet I'm going to clock him with several kilos of salt crystals. But it can't be your response to every situation. You've got to know what action is appropriate."

Amethyst insists that her faith only grows stronger as she gets older. Every day, she takes another step towards being a balanced person; towards improving herself and the world around her.

Though some of her beliefs may seem preposterous, Amethyst is not a madwoman. She holds no illusions about day-to-day life in the modern world. Her faith is actually much more understanding of human nature than many of the major religions. Pop culture images often portray wizards as wise and benevolent, whereas witches are traditionally associated with evil. But why should these ideas affect how we view someone's religious beliefs?

It may seem difficult to believe in some of her more outrageous convictions. But weren't many of humanity's best and brightest regarded as a little eccentric in their time? Perhaps we as a society are too quick to dismiss outlandish beliefs.

There might be something to them after all.

Surface

Clive

It's only fairly recently that our people found out about the rest of the world. The first they knew was when they started experimenting with radio – and discovered that the ether was full of other people's communications. At first nobody realized that that was what all the noise was. I won't bore you with the details of how their languages were deciphered, anyway the fact is I don't really know much beyond the simple stuff about code-breaking that they teach you when you're little.

Then folks began to wonder why the other people weren't picking up our radio and responding to us – that was when they began to realize how big the world is. They were only picking up inter-territory transmissions, and intra-territory transmissions are just too weak to pick up at great distances. Eventually they built a transmitter powerful enough to be heard. They were amazed at how powerful it had to be, and worked out roughly how far away the other territories are. They weren't wildly wrong: the world is only about five times as big as they guessed. This was far less of a surprise than some of the other things the other people have taught us. At first some of them were just plain unbelievable.

In some places, there are *forests*. Forests are like agriculture halls stuffed full of plants, except that the plants are much bigger and tougher, there are no walls or roofs or lights, and they go on for miles and miles and miles. *Up there, on top of the surface!* Probably very interesting places, but certainly very dangerous. No-one lives there, because the forests stop you putting up solar collectors and wind-farms. Just as the coast puts a stop to our territory's expansion in that direction, so some of the other territories are hemmed in by forests. I've seen moving pictures of forests: they're fantastic.

In some places, there are *rivers*. That's lots of water, flowing on the surface. Well, we sort of have rivers in our area – when it rains. But in our area, as soon as the rain stops and all the water's soaked into the ground, that's it. Maybe you didn't know about rain anyway – rain is water falling onto the ground from above, and without it there wouldn't be any water in the ground for us! Or maybe just salt water, soaking in from the sea. But proper rivers flow most of the time, or some of them maybe even *all* the time. I'm not sure why – maybe in those places it rains all the time, or maybe the rain gets stored up somehow and released into the rivers slowly. I don't know.

The territories that have rivers are lucky, because they can *dam* the rivers, and make electricity using them. They call that *hydroelectricity*, and they say it's better than solar collectors and wind farms. Although there are big rivers in some of the forests, it's impossible to dam them for hydroelectricity because the forest just pulls the dams to bits too quickly – the people in one territory have tried several times.

No-one here used to know that the world is round, and spinning! My Dad says that was pretty hard to believe; but of course I've always known, so it seems natural to me.

It was our people who invented railways, and none of the other territories have them. One other place is thinking about trying to make some. Recently, some people from there came in a big boat, and took some of our engineers back to their place to help them.

Boats are amazing. My Mum took me above ground to go and look at it. It was about an hour's walk, above ground, from the end of North Line to where the boat was. It's hard going with the breathing apparatus and carrying your own water; but it was worth it. There was quite a crowd sight-seeing, but I was the only little one, and one of the foreigners spotted me and invited me and my Mum to go onto the boat. We didn't have enough air and water for the extra time, but the foreigner promised to top it up for us so we went. We had to clamber into a little boat that bounced up and down on the sea, because the big boat couldn't come very close to the coast. The little boat was open-topped, so we had to keep our gear on until we got to the big boat. Inside the big boat it was pretty much like home, except that the whole boat is always moving a bit, rocking and swaying about. They say you can't feel any change when it starts to move, but I think that's just because it's always moving. But once a train gets going you don't realize how fast that's going, either.

Boats are ever so slow compared with trains. To the place it came from, it's only about ten times as far as it is from the end of North Line to the end of South East; but they say it takes *four weeks!* Making a boat is a lot of work, too, and they have to carry air, water and food for all the occupants for weeks, so they're very big and expensive to run. There's only three of the seven territories that can be reached by boat so far. Three of the others don't have a coast at all, and the other one is too far away. No-one has mapped the coasts even half as far as that; it's not even certain that the sea goes all the way, there could be a land barrier in between.

My Dad says it's funny to talk about land being a barrier. When he was a boy the sea was the edge of the world. In the other directions you can keep on tunnelling further and further as far as you like, but if you start going under the sea you just get water pouring in unless you put in a ridiculous amount of effort trying to keep it out. In some places they've done it, where the rock is less porous, but in most places it's just not worth it. We don't normally go much below the natural water table even on land, and under the sea the water's salty and no use anyway.

But tunnelling takes years to get anywhere. Boats may be slow compared to trains, but at least they can go somewhere where no-one's ever dug any tunnels.

One of the most fantastic things that oldies are still finding it hard to come to terms with is the idea that once upon a time people used to live out in the open, above ground, without breathing apparatus. In some parts of the world you didn't even need to carry your own water: good clean water was lying about on the surface for the taking! People in one of the territories have folk-tales they claim are from those times, but no-one believed it until some people in one of the other territories found some remains of old structures above ground, and managed to work out something about how people lived in the old days. They reckon that if it was possible to explore up there a bit, there might be quite a lot waiting to be investigated. But they think that mostly the surface has been worn away or mangled by forests since then.

It's hard to imagine the surface getting worn away, really. They say that rainfall and rivers can move the soil pretty quickly in some parts of the world, but why doesn't that just wear it down to bare rock? Experiments show that rock can decompose into soil, but it takes an awful long time. There's even an idea that originally there wasn't any soil, that the forests used to cover more of the world than they do now, and they made the soil, out of rocks. According to the people in one of the territories, in some places you can find remains of forests buried in the ground; they even reckon that the patterns you sometimes find in stone are the remains of ancient forests. How they're supposed to get into the stone is beyond me.

The other thing is that, of the stone patterns I've seen, more look like bones than like any plants I've ever seen – even in pictures of forests. But some of the 'bones' are too big for animal bones, and they aren't like human bones. Some people even think that once upon a time there might have been animals as big as people, or possibly even bigger.

Comparing the history of the different territories is interesting. Three of the territories have been in radio contact for a very long time, but even they have written histories going back much further still. The history of each territory goes back a different distance into the past. One of them goes back over a thousand years, compared to our three hundred.

One interesting conclusion they're beginning to come to is that long before any of them started keeping written histories, we all came from the same place, and that there weren't separate territories at all. Apart from the fact that we're all human and pretty much alike – a few superficial details excepted – whichever territory we come from, all our writing is fairly similar, even if the languages are quite different. Some people who've studied it carefully reckon that even the languages have more in common than you'd expect by chance.

Another part of the argument is that although each territory has its own distinctive technology, most of that has developed within the territory's period of recorded history, and that the ancient core technology is the same in all territories. We all make solar collectors and wind farms in basically the same way. We all make air systems and agricultural lighting in much the same way.

Of course, there may be more territories waiting to be discovered – they just haven't invented radio yet, or they are still in the listening stage. The territories with boats, including us before long maybe, might get into contact with territories with a coast without them developing radio, but it would be easy to miss them anyway. There's not much to see of our territory from the coast, just a few wind farms in the distance; and apparently the boats tend to stay a fair way away from the coast most of the time because there they're at less risk of being bashed into rocks by the movement of the water. The sea is shallow near the edges, but it gets very deep further out.

People in one territory have invented a way of getting about above the ground, that they say could get over any possible land barriers. They call it flying, but it's not much like real flight. They use fixed wings, rather than flapping ones like a bat's or an insect's, and propel themselves with a *rocket*, carrying two

chemicals that react violently together and running
what amounts to a continuous controlled explosion in a
hole at the rear of the vehicle, pushing it forward. The
wings are shaped so as to hold the weight of the craft
on the pressure of air under them. Sounds pretty dodgy,
but apparently it works. It can go nearly as fast as a
train, and even has *more* acceleration. It uses a
phenomenal amount of energy though, and so far
they've only managed to get a few kilometres. Only an
optimist would extrapolate from that to going
thousands of kilometres!

Controlling a flying machine is apparently quite
tricky. They say it's not too bad if the ground's reasonably level where you start and finish, and you don't go
up too high. They've sent animals and instruments up
in rockets that they sent straight up, but they've not
managed to get them back to the ground safely.

In the territory that made the rockets, the sky's
permanently cloudy, so they didn't even know about
the Sun and Moon and stars until they got in touch with
other territories. They must have found that hard to get
to grips with! They don't have a coast, either, so none of
them has ever been to another territory or seen the sky.

A few brave souls here are trying to develop some
kind of agriculture on top of the ground. They flatten
areas and make walls out of slabs of consolidated soil
to prevent rainwater running off so the ground retains
enough moisture for things to grow. Things are indeed
growing, but the ordinary farmers laugh at the
enormous expenditure of effort for so little return.

Anyone would think I was an expert on the sky, and
rain and things. My Mum and Dad are a bit barmy
about The Surface, you see.

Time

Hilary

Squelch-suck – squelch-such – squelch – this time my shoe (a little too big "to allow for growth, madam") had come right off my foot. I sat on the bottom step of the stile between the gate and the spilling cattle-trough and, bracing myself against the gate-post, rocked the shoe till with a smacking grandfatherly kiss the mud parted with it.

It was a sorry sight, cleaned of yesterday's mud with the stump of an old knife only an hour before and cherry-blossomed under Mother's eye. A passion of regret that I had taken the field path to school instead of going round by the lane stung my eyes, but only for a moment. I had plenty of time; Mother had seen to that. And the field path was shorter. I brushed away the tears with the back of my wrist – gritty, slimy, loathsome across my face. Appalled, I looked at my hands, at my shoes, one on, one off, then at the cattle trough. Poor things, I mustn't dirty their drinking water. The horse pond? Its verge was trampled as deep into mud as the gateway itself and, shuddering, I remembered the leeches. Mud-balled shoe in hand, recoiling delicately from sullying the stile's top bar where ladies' skirts would drag, I climbed over and made for the brook.

By the time the water ran clear again after the vigorous splashing of my face and hands and swilling of my shoes, I was at peace with the world. How beautiful and frail my feet were, wavering white under two inches of chattering water among the pebbles I stood on, amber and ivory and garnet, glinting jet on the broken surfaces. I tossed my head, shrugging away the embarrassment of last summer's disappointment at finding that the treasure I had borne home was fairy gold, dry and drab and useless in the morning. Well, I had only been six then. Leave them be; they would stay magical.

I clutched for a hazel branch to steady a sudden lurch; a shower of pollen from the catkins gilded the air. Why "catkins?" Little cats? We called them lambs'-tails. More like. "All hung on a tree to dry!" Bopeep was silly. Would the violets be out? The blue ones were all over the place, but these were special. I crouched along under the silky rabbit-scuts of pussy willow, making for the pool. Pussies with rabbit scuts? I quaked with silent laughter. But then, Old Bill the hedger and ditcher called hares "Puss," didn't he. If I stood still long enough the minnows would come and nibble my legs, kissing me. Here under the cutaway banks the water was deeper, darker, to be treated with hushed reverence for fear of waking – what? But I lingered for the minnows before wading on. My shoes, hung round my neck on knotted laces, were pouring muddy water down my frock in little spurts.

Coins of sunlight slid warm over my skin under the tasselled hazels as I came out from the green gloom of the willows round the pool. There, sheltering beneath the dogs mercury on the bank, I found my violets, my delicate blue-veined darlings. I picked some for my teacher, only three, with a few leaves, to let the others seed for next year, as Father had taught me. I wound a long grass round the stems to make a posy and smelled them in a rapture.

Teacher.

What time was it?

I listened. No bird song; they were all too busy feeding their families. No farming sounds. Worse, no playground screams.

They must have gone in.

Galloping the last half mile, swishing down the green cart lane regardless of young nettles, threading the larch spinney, across the playground (the chanting of times tables loud through the open windows) I crept into school, into "the big room" I had been promoted to last September. A silence fell, fifteen pairs of eyes fixed upon me. I held out my fragile little offering. "Teacher" was new at Christmas, a war widow, unhappy, town-bred and longing for home. She struck the desk with her cane.

I flushed hotly. Was this going to happen to me? Poor Sid and Perce often felt that vicious sting, poor little chaps, "not the full shilling," Father said. I had flinched and wept for them. And for others. But me?

No.

"What sort of time do you think this is?" she squawked, angry red patching her face and neck. "Just look at the clock – you can read the time, I suppose!"

I looked at the round face on the far wall. My arm sank to my side, the posy slipping from my stunned fingers. How did it come to be half past ten?

"Can't your mother get you up in the morning? And just look at you! How dare she send you to school like that! Tell her from me to wash your frock occasionally and give you a bath. You're all mud – it's disgusting!

And you a farmer's daughter! I know I can't expect anything from the labourers' children and them from the brickyard, but you! With your airs and graces and this book and that book! Stand in front of the class."

I was going to be sent to Coventry, mortified by boys I had learned to feel sorry for. And the girls would be worse. My ribs closed inwards. I held my face taut and high, staring unseeing at the clock.

She stood above me, the violets screaming silently under her wicked high-heeled London shoes, and wrenched a cluster of catkins from my tousled head. "Ugh!" she hissed, bending close. "Washed your face and left a tidemark! Think you're somebody! In the army they call that "dumb insolence.""

How the tatterdemalions in the back row were enjoying this.

"Face the blackboard. Now, stay there."

I did. For an hour and a half, all through playtime and sum time and – worst of all – reading time for everyone who had finished. I suddenly remembered my dinner bag, packed so lovingly and so unheedingly left – where? By the stile? The brook? Long before home time some creature would have found it, mice, ants, a fox perhaps. The class whispered and fidgeted. Pages turned. Nibs jarred into inkwells. Would the morning never end? The rosemary savour and melting crispness of my mother's mutton pasty and the wrinkled sweetness of the last of the apples possessed my mind. The clock ticked, slower and slower; I dared not turn my head to look at it.

The twelve o'clock hooter wailed from the brickyard, time for our release, labourers and scholars both. Tottering a little, I wandered into the playground and sat on the stump where Old Jack split the firewood for the big iron boiler. My shoes were nearly dry, crusted into a vengeful harshness that cut into my feet when I had at last forced them on. The brickyard children had all run home for their dinners. I could expect no mercy, much less a spare crust from the sandwich-munchers. Should I run home? Better not, that would be a double disgrace. What had clocks to do with time, I wondered, or time with clocks? Very little, I decided, for how long, how very long already it had been since I reached school that morning. And how unimaginably long were the hours now stretching between my small and hungry self and the joyful scampered mile that would bring me home.

And Time Again

Hilary

I was back from the kitchen with my can of hot water before the alarm clock was due and remembered to cut it off before it set my nerves jangling along with it. Of course I hadn't slept – and couldn't bear to stay in bed – how could I? It was seven years to the day, a bright morning, just such another as this, a fresh Spring morning after a night of rain, that the telegram had arrived. And within the year the Armistice came, too late for Gerald. Too late for me.

We had our eye on an exceptionally nice little house in Ravenscourt Park, handy for the Underground and his work, near the shops, a secluded little garden, safe to play in. He looked forward so much to having children, bless him.

I wonder if I would have lost my baby if he hadn't been killed. No point wondering. He wanted a boy, of course, planned to call him Gerald. But she'd've been a girl anyway, if she had lived.

My rib still hurts where I caught it on the beastly swing-arm towel rail of that gimcrack washstand, horrid thing, all flaky white paint over the rust, looks like a mantrap until you put the basin in. And that's insanitary, too, and the can that goes with it, all chipped along the blue enamel rim. Disgusting. I hate them. Mrs. Cooper could at least provide a proper marble-topped washstand and a decent china set, if modern sanitation is out of the question, that is. Worst of all I hate the slop pail and the earth closet down the garden. There was a nice bathroom in the Ravenscourt Park house, unlimited hot water from an up-to-date geyser and a water closet right alongside, upstairs, very nice, with a mahogany seat.

Mrs. Cooper hasn't even got gas.

Still, I could do worse, I suppose. Her house is clean and her cooking's not bad. Unfortunately the man who has the attic room works in the cornmarket, not my type really. But we only have to meet at tea. He goes off before me in the mornings; my train doesn't go until ten past eight and we're right by the station. I'm lucky to have a post at all, but they are extremely short of teachers, so many of the men having … Not that I would ever have considered being a shop girl. Or a nurse – not that, oh no.

Oh Gerald, Gerald. They told me it was instantaneous, that you didn't suffer – though what you'd been doing for three years in that case I don't know – At least you didn't hang about in a field dressing station waiting to die. Or dangle in the barbed wire. A clean death they said. How could it be clean? It's always the mud that they talk about, when you can get them to talk at all that is. Was it face down in the mud, my darling, with all the boots clomping and slithering? That's my worst nightmare still.

Never mind the early start, I still nearly missed the train. The guard saw me running and held the flag for me, didn't blow the whistle until I was safely in. A nice man, fortyish. I wonder, was he in the trenches or were guards essential services? That train simply dawdles; I almost believe it when they say the driver has the fireman walking alongside making daisy chains. There was a woman opposite me, staring. "What's up with you, Mrs. Penfold?" she asked. I must have been looking pretty wretched. "It's just seven years since St. Quentin," I said. She stared some more. "Your husband?" I nodded. Then, "Seven years is a long time." A long time! What does she know about it? How did she know my name anyway? I don't remember setting eyes on her before. The children point you out, I suppose, like they would royalty – or a cripple.

I got out at the halt. Talk about Shakespeare's schoolboy, "unwillingly to school" – he had nothing on me. There was a primrose in the bank by the lane; I vaguely remembered something about "pin-eye" and "thrum-eye;" I could do a lesson on that if I got the children to bring some in. I bent to see which kind this primrose was and found it was all splattered with mud. Horrible! Better leave it alone, anyway. It's tempting fate to try pandering to their rural interests; the time I drew a cow on the blackboard, quite a good drawing it was, too, although I say it, and asked them what it was, that uppity little miss asked "could it be an Ayrshire," whatever that is, and when I said surely they knew a cow when they saw one, she said wasn't it more of a heifer, I felt my colour rise and then the whole hue and cry began – Heifers and stirks and bulls and bullocks – and what that meant, which I didn't want to know about – and that led on to sweetbreads somehow (I'll never eat another!) and stallions and geldings and hogs and how "hoggs" (which Miss Goody Two Shoes had to spell out for me of course) were not pigs but sheep. I was terribly upset. Children can be so cruel. Always trying to put me right, that child. And to look at her you'd think butter wouldn't...

Mrs. Winter was there before me, getting ready for her half dozen little ones. They seem to love her, but I don't think they learn much. How can they? She's only half-educated herself. Drums their letters into them, most of them, which is just as well. If they can't read by the time I get them how am I meant to teach them anything? How much good I can do them anyway I often wonder, poor little souls. That's if I stay. Or if they keep me on. Please God, I need this post, any post!

At least, it being so fine, we didn't have to put up with filthy floors and the stink of wet wool all morning. I could even have the windows open to disperse the unlovely odour of unwashed children, some of whom had clearly slept in their clothes, poor little scraps. I do truly feel for them, though I must confess my gorge does rise at that stuff from their noses all over their top lips and scabs and rashes and things. And the smell. I thought that was what you got in the East End slum schools, which I'd opted out of in favour of the "lovely country." I could tell the picture book people a thing or two. What was it that poet said?

Here in the country's heart

Where the grass is green

Life is the same sweet life…

He can't have known much about it.

Little-Miss-Ever-Helpful hadn't come; I could get on with routine. Even that boy Sidney sat still during Scripture, scratching himself through the tear in his short trousers, and did his spellings after a fashion. I don't mind admitting I'm actually somewhat frightened of that boy, such a big brute, eyes on a level with mine when he looks at me under those heavy brows. If I didn't keep the cane handy he'd never do a thing I say. And there's no help within reach; we're all women here, apart from poor old Jack, who left that leg in Bloemfontein apparently. If it came to it we'd be no match for a boy like Sidney; he's an animal. But he was chanting his seven times along with the others when she decided to waltz in at very nearly playtime, grinning all over her face and pushing some wretched weed or other at me as a peace offering. Well, she couldn't soft soap me, not that morning of all mornings. She was covered in mud, reeked of it, standing there in an oblong of sunlight, oblong like a grave, standing there all covered in mud in a grave of sunlight, smiling like the Sun smiled on the fields of St. Quentin that morning. Never said a word, just stood there. Dumb insolence they call it in the army. I told her. Dumb insolence.

How I got her out of there I really do not know, or how I got through the rest of the morning with her like a little effigy somewhere behind my left shoulder. Oh Gerald, my Gerald, this is not like me, you wouldn't even recognize me if you came back – I'm only thirty-four, for heaven's sake, and I'm turning into a bitter old woman who can't love children any more because I'm afraid of them and I have to keep them down. I don't want to hit children! I hate being unkind but what can I do? I'm trapped, my darling, as deep in the mud as ever you were, and the harder I try to get out the more I flounder.

And in a few weeks' time we'll all be jolly saluting the flag for Empire Day and next November the eleventh there'll be another bloody two minutes' silence.

The Farmer and the Wolf

John

Part I

So you want a story, do you? So what would you like to hear?

Something about Wolves?

And Tigers?

Both of them together? Well, that's a bit of a stretch, but I do happen to know one story that might please you. Well, maybe; it all depends on which you like best out of wolves and tigers, I suppose.

Once, many years ago, but not so many that I can't remember it as if it were yesterday, there was a farmer who lived in India. Now don't go an-asking what part of India he lived in, as it don't rightly matter.

In point of fact, our friend the farmer didn't really know or care what part of India he lived in. All he knew was his farm, the nearby village where he sold his produce, and his wife & little daughter, who he loved more than anything else in the world.

He was thinking of them that evening as he walked home from the market, his sack slung over his shoulder – filled with food for the larder, trinkets for his wife and toys for his girl – and a lit lantern in his hand. He'd had a good days selling his crop, and now made his way back to the farm, a spring in his step and a whistle upon his lips.

But a commotion caught his attention, just off the main path and a little way into the scrub. There was a frightful sound of roaring and growling. Now, our farmer friend was no fool, and was usually as cautious as cautious can be, but something in the sounds made him stop. "maybe I should go and see what's causing the noise" he thought to himself.

Quietly moving through the bushes, what a sight was before him! a sorely wounded she-wolf, standing guard over two wolf cubs. And in front of her... well, the farmers heart froze in fear in his chest. In front of her stalked a huge Tiger, gazing hungrily at the she-wolf's cubs through malicious eyes.

Now, tigers can be magnificent beasts, but that's what they are – beasts. Vicious killers and takers of whatever they want. They consider themselves lords of the jungle; and there aren't many as can gainsay them. I'm sure there may be some that might leave well enough alone, but this tiger seemed to be cruelly playing with the she-wolf, seemingly gaining pleasure out of seeing the wolf get weaker and weaker; knowing that soon she must fail and fall, and her young would be his meal.

Our friend the farmer took all this scene in as he crouched beside the bush. He saw the courage of the she wolf, and thought about what he might do to protect his own daughter if he were in the wolf's place.

He'd never been so close to a tiger before, and to tell it true, was scared almost witless; but he knew he couldn't let this be. All the same he was as probably as startled as the tiger, when he found himself rushing at the beast, screaming and whirling his lantern around his head!

The tiger turned, suddenly surprised, and was rewarded by a lantern full of oil catching it full on the side of its jaw. The oil spilled out, covering the tiger's face, and instantly caught fire! The tiger let out an agonized roar, whirling on the spot, trying to desperately put out the flames, and quench the agony that engulfed its head.

The she-wolf, sensing a chance, girded herself for a final effort and launched herself upon the tiger, her jaws reaching for the tigers throat! But the tiger, even in the midst of blinding pain lashed out with one giant paw, and the wolf was thrown to the side.

But she had done enough. The tiger fled into the jungle; its roar sounding almost like a pitiful scream rather than the sound that would normally fill the jungle with terror.

Our farmer friend could not believe what he had done – he had faced a tiger... he had *burned* a tiger, and made it flee! – but his joy and triumph quickly faded when he saw the wolf. His heart wrenched with pity as he saw her try to rise and reach her cubs, but her legs failed her, and she sank to the ground, almost spent and near to death.

Once again the farmer acted without thinking. He ran over to the cubs, picked them up and carried them over to their mother. Their worried yelping roused her, and with a strength that broke his heart to see, she licked and reassured the cubs. Then she looked at our friend the Farmer, and he realized that both she and her cubs had mismatched eyes – one golden, and one blue. But more: her gaze seemed to bare him down to his very soul – and in that gaze seemed to be an unspoken request.

For to a wolf, the pack is all, and the wellbeing of the young is more important than anything else. And so it was that the farmer knew what she was asking of him, and he knew he could not refuse. With a simple nod of the head he agreed. The she wolf – in turn – licked his hand, as if in thanks; and that was her last act in life.

The farmer took the two wolf cubs home to his wife and daughter, and together, they raised them as part of the family. But wolves – as you and I and everyone knows – aren't meant to live under a roof, and after a year the farmer knew that for their sake, he had to let them run free. Her taught them as best he could how to hunt and stalk, but soon knew that he couldn't teach them anything more, and they would have to go their own way.

So he took them into the jungle, and he let them go. as they reached the edge of the clearing, they both turned and looked at the farmer, their mismatched eyes gleaming in the sunlight. And then they were gone, never to be seen again.

Or so the farmer thought.

What's that? No way to end a story?

WELL!

Well, if that was the end of the story then perhaps you might have a complaint against me. However that ain't the end of the story; but it's all I'll be telling tonight. Maybe tomorrow night I'll tell the rest; but tonight the fire's burning low and it's time to turn in.

Sweet dreams, my precious ones. Sleep well, and maybe dream of wolves.

And of a farmer, who had faced a tiger, and his fear, and stood his ground and overcame both.

Part II

Well that's a nice fire you got going there, Shift over a bit, you're hogging the good spot. Reckon the smoke'll go more the other way now that I've moved; ah well.

Anyway, who's for a story? I've got a good one about a brave Knight called Sir Dennis and a Troll Bridge... No? All right, how about the dread Wyrm of Lambton? That's a good 'un! Yes, I know I told that one last week, but I thought perhaps...

I know, I know… you want to hear about the farmer don't you? The one from last night; him, the wolves and the tiger. Well, I suppose I could finish that one off. Now where was I?

So, here we are back in India, and a few years have passed. The Farmer still plows his furrow at his little farmstead, with his wife and daughter beside him. He still goes to the market in the nearby village to sell his crops, and still comes home from there with food for the larder, trinkets for his wife, and toys for his little girl. She's that little bit older now, walking and talking, and doing all those things that little girls do.

Like her father, she misses the two wolf pups that our friend had taken in, and she wishes she could see them again. You see, she still sees them as the cubs they were, playfully running around her, yipping and licking at her laughing face. She's still too young to think what they might have grown into.

But every night, she puts out two saucers of milk for them, just she used to, hoping that one day they would come home.

Well, it was market day again, and our friend the farmer had decided to bring his little girl into town with him, so she could see the bright lights and all the fancy townsfolk. Their day had been well spent, the farmer selling his wares, whilst his girl drank in the sites and sounds whilst sitting in the shade of the large tree in the middle of the market square. But time passes as it always must, and soon the sun was low in the sky, and it was time to make their way home.

Our friend the farmer walked along, his sack slung over his shoulder, and his little girl tightly holding his hand as they made their way down the path home. But it wasn't long before the farmer started to feel somehow uneasy. his eyes shifted this way and that, and his ears alert to any sound out of the ordinary. And then he saw it.

There, in the undergrowth just off the path, a movement; a shape, a flicker of yellow and black. And then, through a break in the leaves, the unmistakable glare of a bright yellow eye. The farmer's heart started to pound, a sweat came upon his brow, and his breath came in light bursts. A tiger was stalking them!

"Come along my Love!" he called to his daughter, trying not to let the worry show in his voice, "Let's brisken up our pace. Mother will be waiting for us." He was careful to keep his body between the hidden tiger and his daughter, and together they walked that bit faster.

And the tiger kept pace with them.

"Come along, my love, let me carry you; I can see that the day has worn you out" The Framer lifted his daughter into his arms, and his pace became brisker yet. His heart pounding, his eyes never leaving the undergrowth.

And still, the tiger kept pace with them.

Just then his little girl cried out, and our friend was sure she must have spotted the tiger. But no, her gaze fell on the other side of the track, and she pointed into the undergrowth there. The farmer stole a quick glance that way and his heart leapt in his chest.

For there, in the bushes, was another tiger.

Keeping pace with them.

"Close your eyes Darling, close them and hold tight!" The farmer started to run as fast as his legs could carry him along the path, his girl clinging to his neck as hard as she could.

Yet somehow they must have taken a wrong turn, for the farmer was brought up abruptly when he realized that he had run into a clearing, and there was no other way out! And from the under bushes they came, those two tigers, stalking leisurely forwards, their eyes never leaving our friend and his little girl.

It was then that our friend saw it. One tiger – the larger off the two – one side of its face was hideously burnt, and that side's eye was a ruined hole. The farmer suddenly remembered a clearing, a she-wolf, and him striking at the tiger she was fighting with his lantern. The oil spilling out and setting alight the tiger's face.

And he knew, there and then, why this tiger was stalking him and his daughter.

Revenge.

And there we'll leave them for the moment, as I need to take care of some business behind that tree. Oh don't look at me like that – you'll get your tale's end tonight;

but even stories must wait when nature calls. Save my spot by the fire, it's cold out there!

Part III(a)

Ah, that's so much better – and you left me my space! Anyone would think there was something you was after from me. Anyway, who's for a song to cheer us all up? ALL RIGHT – I'm just joshing with you; it's time to find out how our story ends. Ahem…

The tigers killed and et them…

OUCH!!!! Don't you be throwing pine cones at me, young fella me lad! I can throw them back, and I've a darn sight better aim than you do! Anyways, here's what really happened...

Part III(b)

In the clearing everything seemed so still. Our friend the farmer standing in the middle, holding tightly to his little girl. Standing before them were the two tigers; one with a burnt face and the other – smaller – one seemingly taking its lead from the old burnt face one. With soft growls, the two tigers started to approach, and the farmer knew then for certain that all hope was lost.

But then there came a howling from behind the farmer – the howling of wolves – and the tigers hesitated. His little girl cried out again, only this time not in fear, but with joy:

"They've come back! Papa, they've come back to us!"

Sure enough, from out of the bush behind them came two wolves; their pace unhurried; their mismatched eyes – one golden and one blue – fixed steadily and fearlessly upon the tigers. They walked around our friend the farmer, and then stood there in the middle between the farmer & his daughter and the tigers. For to a wolf, the pack is all, and the safety of the young is more important than anything else.

So who moved first? The tigers? the wolves? Our friend? Who knows? I certainly don't. All I know is all of a sudden the tigers were springing forward, and the wolves darted around them, howling their defiance. Everything was happening so quick that the farmer could hardly make sense, so he held his little girl tightly, determined that she should not be touched whilst there was breath in his body.

Now tigers and wolves fight in different ways. Tigers are strength and brute force, seeking to overpower their prey. But wolves are tricksy, relying on speed and cunning. One wolf would dance in front of a tiger, and the other would nip past and attack the tiger from behind. – quick as that! And normally, wolves working together as a pack would be a match for a tiger.

But of course there was more than one tiger in the clearing.

As the wolves fought the smaller tiger, the Burntface one turned its attention to our friend the farmer; hatred and fury in its one good eye. The farmer stared around, looking for something to arm himself with, and then remembered something. he reached into his sack, bought out his lantern and started swinging it at old Burntface. The tiger saw the lantern and flinched as if remembering how it had got so very badly scarred. But this only lasted a moment, and old Burntface crouched, ready to spring at our friend.

But before it could spring, a great howl rang through the glade. The two wolves looked up, and joined their voices to the wolfsong. And both tigers paused, suddenly confused.

For suddenly standing there, between old Burntface and the Farmer – where nothing had been before – was another wolf! This wolf was much larger than the two, but had the same mismatched eyes, one golden, and one blue. And the Farmer realized, with an absolute certainty, that he had seen this She-wolf before

The wolf stood there calmly watching old Burntface, The farmer could not believe his eyes, for he was sure that the wolf was glowing! It was like it somehow wasn't quite there; but at the same time was more real than the ground beneath his feet.

Then the She-wolf sprang at old Burntface with a terrible purpose in her every movement. To a wolf, the pack is all, and the safety of the young is more important than anything else; perhaps even more important than death itself. Old Burntface jumped back, seeming terror in its every movement, but it was no good. The she-wolf sprang at Burntface's throat, and this time there was no paw fast enough to swat her away. She struck, sure and deadly and then leaped away. Burntface reared up, tottered, and the fell to the ground, as dead as dead can be.

Burntface lay on the ground as still as a rock and blood pooling around its body. The younger tiger panicked, and that moment of fatal hesitation gave the two wolves all that they needed to finish their deadly, grisly work.

And then it was over.

The three wolves, the she wolf flanked by her two grown cubs, came to the farmer. The two younger wolves went to the farmers daughter, yelping and panting like puppies, and licking the tears of relief from her delighted face. The she-wolf simply faced our friend, and he stared back, all fear gone. He raised his open hand, and she allowed him to stroke her; and then his arms were around her and the tears flowed freely from his eyes.

However, all things have their time, and all times must finally pass. After a moment or two the she-wolf gently, but firmly moved away from the farmer, and walked toward the edge of the clearing. As if by an unspoken signal her two grown cubs left the farmers little girl and joined their mother.

The three of them turned once more to face our friend the farmer & his daughter, and raised their heads for one final howl. As the howl faded, there were but two wolves at the edge of the clearing: their mother was gone. She had repaid her debt to the farmer, and could once again rest. Then the two wolves turned, and made their way into the undergrowth, and were rapidly gone from sight.

So our Friend the Farmer took his little girl by the hand, and led her away from the glade, and back home, where his wife was waiting by the door.

To a wolf, the pack is all, and the Safety of the young is more important than anything else.

And a wolf always repays their debts.

Bunker 2.6

Stephen

It would be fair to say that at this point the reality of their situation has still not fully hit our Dwellers. Or if it has they have indulged in some rather monumental denial.

Small moments here and there perhaps. The odd bizarre craving or maybe the distant feeling of missing something important. But as yet the newness has trumped the really rather dreadful day to day realness of it all. Each of them having the odd flash, although as yet only once resulting in anything spectacular.

But Desmond's inner monologue during the argument has pointed out to him a reality that had previously escaped his notice. As things stood, right in this very moment. Zahid was the happiest of all of them. His blissful lack of knowledge giving him something the other Dwellers will never again have. Hope.

Yes, he was incarcerated in a room not much bigger than his dad's old shed. But weren't they too trapped in a cell? Ok so it had a bit more leg room and a few more toys… and better food. But realistically how was his current situation any worse than being trapped in the Bunker proper? And then an even worse thought. Would killing him be doing him a favour?

Desmond's fragile ego recoiled from that thought before it went any further.

Unfortunately it's at this point in the conversation that Desmond found himself saying –

Desmond – I suppose he could top himself, you know, in grief.

And a stark reality dawned on him. It was such a deeply unpleasant thought that he immediately tucked it away. But it does at least explain his rather fatalistic, some would say Driven demeanour.

And so the four dwellers are making their way to the detention centre. They rather rapidly fall into pairs with one dropping back while the other accelerates forward. At least one person in each pair has done this on purpose to enable them to talk privately. Both are feeling the need to be subtle so it's rather a shame that everyone knows exactly whats going on. The pairs are utterly predictable.

Mary – I cant believe that you're considering this, he's a human being.

Colin – Doesn't matter does it?

Mary – What? How can that not matter?

Colin – Well, if we leave him in there, then the worst that happens is he lives in cell for the rest of his life. However long that may be.

Mary – But that's horrific.

This makes Colin stop for a moment and motion at the walls.

Colin – Really? If we let him out and he turns out to be a nutter and kills someone?

Mary – We cant assume that he's bad

Colin – Based on your distrust of the source. Who's distrust is more important here? If you're right all's well. If you're wrong someone dies. But the worst thing that happens if we leave him in there is… what?

Mary takes a moment to process this. For a start she's sure she's had this argument before, including Colin's slightly stoned delivery. She's almost certain she won easily when she was debating with stoned philosophy students. But somehow, this time, it wasn't going so smoothly. She considers this may be due to a number of things. Not least the fact that Colin's judgement, while chemically affected, is not being swayed by the need to get into her pants. But she's forced to admit to herself that the reality of the situation makes arguing her side that much harder. All well and good arguing basic human decency when all you have is righteousness to consider and not someone's, possibly your own, life.

She's also shaken by having to argue against Colin at all. Till now she had assumed he would naturally support her position. Meanwhile, up ahead.

Desmond – I'm right in thinking only your key opens the cells? Right?

Howard – I haven't the faintest idea. I do know with my key I can shut off his resources, including air.

Desmond takes a moment to consider both this and the slightly bitter tone with which it is delivered. Whereas Howard's long lost working class sensibility's are once more being kindled. Sadly, Desmond has no awareness of this and proceeds to fan the flames.

Desmond – Wow really?

Howard– I can deny resources to any of the rooms, below the command level.

Desmond makes a quick mental calculation.

Desmond – So, not the Officers' Quarters then?

Howard – No. Apparently not.

Desmond – Oh, well, I mean the cells would be 'Lower Floors' so to speak

Howard – Safe to assume, but Colin's 'Commander' key may be able to change that.

Desmond – So if we are going to keep this guy locked up we are going to have to do something about Colin...

The two stop in the corridor and look at each other. Desmond is trying to give off an aura of quiet command. But something about Howard's barely contained fury suggests to him it's not working.

Howard – So as well as killing this bloke in the cells you'll be needing me to 'Off' Colin too?

Desmond – Well I think that's a bit harsh, but we may need to take his key off him at least. I mean, look at them.

He gestures down the corridor at Colin and Mary having their own heated debate further down the corridor.

Desmond – No doubt plotting what they are going to do when we get there.

Even the worst people watcher could see that they were not planning but in fact arguing. Whereas actual plotting was, it seemed, going down right under his nose.

Desmond – We can't let their dodgy hippy principles put all of us at risk.

Howard – So sod democracy is it?

Desmond – Well no, but obviously we can't risk this being voted on, a fifty fifty will just cause more arguments. And I can't see head office taking their side on this one, we will be forced to take arbitrary action sooner or later. It's inevitable.

Howard – Inevitable.

Desmond – With respect Howard, ten minutes ago you seemed happy to walk down here and deal with this on your own.

All four dwellers arrive at the Detention centre at the same time. After a moment's umming they defer to Howard who opens the doors with his key.

The Detention Centre is a simple affair. It was never considered that a large prison would be needed. It's probably best we don't think too deeply about why. Its layout would be familiar to any scifi geek or even for that matter any western fan. A large fixed desk with a comfortable chair facing four box like cells. Each cell, rather than a window, has a monitor over the door showing its contents. These reveal two things. Firstly, Zahid, who is watching his own in-cell monitor which is also showing him. And secondly, in another cell, a corpse.

All four of them take in this sight. They look at the corpse without comment, but in fairness to them, they had all seen corpses on screen before. Once more taking his chosen leadership role Desmond takes a step forward and examines the controls. After a brief moment he flicks a switch.

Desmond – Hello?

The effect is instantly trippy as Zahid's image, multiplied into infinity leaps off his bed and looks around anxiously. He speaks but they can't hear him.

Mary – Look at him, we *have* to let him out.

Desmond – We in fact don't.

Mary – We Can Not leave him in there to die!

Desmond – Mary, we cannot have a security risk walking around the base willy nilly.

Mary – So you're ok with us all becoming jailers are you?

Desmond – On the contrary, keeping him alive would be a waste of valuable resources, Howard can just turn off his air.

Colin taps Desmond's arms a few times and nods at the screen. It is immediately clear that Zahid can hear them talking. He is staring at the camera with a shocked and pitiful look on his face.

Howard pushes Desmond aside and turns off the mike.

Howard – So we all become Jailers or I become a murderer?

Desmond – Well, I mean, murderer is a bit harsh. We'd be putting him out of his misery really.

Howard – Except we wouldn't, I would.

Desmond – Well if your having moral issues then I'm sure we can talk to the Recc One and I'm equally sure they will be able to do it remotely.

Both Mary and Colin have taken a step back as Desmond and Howard have now properly squared off.

Colin – I'm pretty sure they can't do that actually, I'm certain it would have to be done at this end.

Desmond – Well, I mean if it's just about flicking a switch then I'm sure you can be relieved of *that* responsibility Howard.

Mary has been examining the controls. She leans over the desk and flicks another two switches.

Zahid – …… I wish I'd never visited now, but Dad said it were traditional. I mean how traditional can it be when it involves a jet engine I said, but he wouldn't listen. An it was a few weeks of mi college course missed, and professor Nells said I was one of his best students. But I didn't know! Can I just speak to mi mum, I wont tell her where I am I swear……

She flicks the switches off again and Zahid's Brummie squeak is silenced once more. They all stare at the monitor for a moment. Desmond coughs.

Desmond – Well clearly this is way too big a decision for us, we need to talk to Recc one.

Mary – So you can have some orders to follow?

Once again she flicks the switches.

Zahid – ….. An he said 'Yeah sure' so we went out into the hills, I didn't know we were crossing the border, there's no dotted line or owt. But it was that or fix his dad's car and I fancied seeing how it was grown....

And off again.

Desmond – Yes Mary, and at the very least because this situation requires some serious thought and perhaps advice from wiser heads.

Colin nods his agreement and leaves the room a slight look of concern on his face. Mary, satisfied for the moment that nothing was going to happen to Zahid at least also nods and follows Colin out of the room.

Desmond – Yes?

Howard – Aye, you go with them and ask Recc One and I'll stay here and keep an eye out in case anyone does anything stupid.

Desmond – Good idea

It dawns on Desmond that he and Howard are in rather close proximity. He pats Howard on the chest, aware of how feeble a gesture it is and with a conspiratorial nod he follows the other two out of the Detention centre. Howard watches them go on the external monitor and eventually when they leave his sight he nods satisfied. He then walks over to Zahid's cell door and opens it.

Howard – You can fix cars?

Human Contact

Jack

She comes here every day.

Of all the places in the city, the plaza is Olurell's favourite. She's sitting halfway up her favourite set of steps, watching the light refracting from the curved glass towers, and shimmering from the wide rectangular pools that run across its length. When she closes her eyes, she can hear the low hubbub of people mingling with the faint, distant rush of traffic. A soft, enveloping blanket of sound.

But something's wrong.

It's a faint flutter on the edge of her consciousness, something she's learned never to ignore.

Someone is watching her.

Olurell looks to her left, just in time to catch his eye. He's sitting a few feet away, along the same step as her. He winks. She looks away, keeping her eyes fixed on the water. Calm. She has to stay calm. A shadow passes over her. He's blocking her light.

"Mind if I sit here?"

Yes. YES! No – calm.

She looks up and smiles. "Sure."

He sits down beside her, resting his forearm on one knee. He's young, attractive; at ease. All Collectors are.

"Just wonderful, isn't it?" he sighs.

Just breathe normally. Breathe. Don't let him see.

"It's beautiful." she agrees. Her scars are itching. She runs her tongue over her incisors. Blunt.

Human.

"Do you live here?"

He doesn't know. Everything's fine.

"Close by." she says, fighting to keep her voice steady.

He turns to smile at her. "I do envy you."

His eyes are brown. The last Collector's had been blue. She remembers how they bulged from their sockets when she drove the Lightblade into his throat.

"Are you here on your own?"

He asks the question lightly, but she can hear the edge in his voice. He's close enough to lunge at her, but she can feel the cool metal of the hilt in her left hand, out of his sight. She's faster now.

Stronger. No hesitating this time.

Do it.

She can see stubble under his chin; he hasn't shaved this morning.

You have to kill him now.

Does he live alone? Do the Collectors even have families?

I'm not going back...

Something changes in his face, and he jerks back as if he's been struck.

"I'm sorry – you want to be on your own."

Olurell says nothing, knuckles white on the grip. He gets up quickly, his composure gone.

"Sorry, I hope I – sorry."

She watches him walk across the plaza. A minute passes. Then her breath comes flooding out of her in bursts, her heart pounding hard enough to make her feel sick. She can suddenly feel the tracks of the tears on her face. She was about to kill him. Murder him. Just a random stranger.

It's dangerous here, she realizes. *She's* dangerous. Even if the Collectors don't find her here, she still can't be near people. She has to move again. Go, run. Find another continent. Maybe even another planet.

Olurell takes a deep breath, steadying herself. Then she stands up, and walks away from the water.

She doesn't look back.

Remarkable Dust of Sand

Lovie

When you feel insignificant
as if you're only just a grain of sand,
a microscopic particle
whom nobody notices
Maybe you're a granule in a desert,
a pellet on a river bottom,
a spark of light
or a gliding fragment
in a sunlit dusty room…

When you're feeling frail
as if the slightest windblow
could sweep you away
and you think you're worthless
Ease your senses and remember
how you beat the odds
when you came to exist
and how wonderful it is
to have life's mysteries
to ponder about
all the good
and all the bad
are opportunities
to learn and evolve

Remember that you have
a voice of your own,
a life only you can lead

Don't ever lend that power
to anyone else
Only you can play your part
Don't wait,
you have everything you need
it's all within you

The Authors

Some of us are, or were, family; we're all friends. Some of us were at school together in the 1960s, or were house-mates in the 1970s.

Some of us only know each other online, through *deviantart.com*, an art community, through friends of friends on *facebook*, or through *justthetalk.com*, a forum that was originally a sort of lifeboat for survivors of the sinking of the good ship *Guardian User Talk*, a forum created by the Guardian newspaper for its readers and then, after a few years, summarily destroyed by them for Reasons Apparently Best Left Obscure.

Our ages range from the mid-twenties to – well, Hilary was a month short of ninety-five when she died in June 2016.

Most of us are native English speakers, but Lovie's mother-tongue is Icelandic, and Anuj's is Marathi. We all wrote in English.

One of Harry's pieces, like his piece in Different Minds Different Lives, is a true one – England, 1943. Anuj's pieces are straight recounts of his own experiences. Vince says you can decide for yourself whether his is a recount or a story or a bit of both.

Different Minds Different Lives

ISBN 978-3-942357-26-5

Kaleidoscope is a companion volume to *Different Minds Different Lives* – an earlier book of short stories also published by Xin Publishing, featuring many of the same authors and an equally eclectic selection of stories.

If you've enjoyed *Kaleidoscope*, make sure to get its companion volume to delve into the world of *Different Minds Different Lives...*